A Tomato Can Chronicle

See page 72

A Tomato Can Chronicle

AND OTHER STORIES OF FISHING AND SHOOTING

EDMUND WARE SMITH
ILLUSTRATED BY RALPH L. BOYER

LYONS
PRESS

Essex, Connecticut

LYONS
PRESS

An imprint of Globe Pequot, the trade division of
The Rowman & Littlefield Publishing Group, Inc.
4501 Forbes Blvd., Ste. 200
Lanham, MD 20706
www.rowman.com

Distributed by NATIONAL BOOK NETWORK

British Library Cataloguing in Publication Information available

Library of Congress Cataloging-in-Publication Data

ISBN 978-1-4930-7297-2 (paperback)
ISBN 978-1-4617-0827-8 (e-book)

∞™ The paper used in this publication meets the minimum requirements of
American National Standard for Information Sciences—Permanence of Paper for
Printed Library Materials, ANSI/NISO Z39.48-1992.

TO HENRY S. DENNISON,
WITH GRATITUDE, AFFECTION,
AND SOMETHING AKIN TO AWE

CONTENTS

ILLUSTRATIONS

FOREWORD

I HAVE known my father-in-law so long that his eccentricities no longer seem eccentric. But I cannot truthfully deny that his behavior, like his mind, is frequently exciting and original. Therefore I am no more than mildly resentful when some good friend, who knows him little, expresses amazement at an act or utterance which to the friend seems unexplainable.

I remember the shocked expression on Dr. M.'s face one time when I met him shortly after he had visited my father-in-law. "I came in the front door," Dr. M. said, "and there he stood in the living room, with nothing on but moccasins and a pair of old khaki pants. His chest and torso were literally covered with green birch lice. He had an axe and a bush-hook in one hand, and a copy of Perry's *Present Philosophical Tendencies* in the other."

"What's puzzling about that?" I asked the Doctor.

"It isn't what you'd expect of a man of his station, when you have just heard he had a lame shoulder."

FOREWORD

"I can explain all," I told the Doctor. "His shoulder got well. He went out on the hill to cut wire birches, and took the book along to read when he was resting. It was hot, so he took off his shirt."

"But why was he cutting birches?"

"He likes it. The only possible objection I see to his indulgence is that he occasionally misses a birch and hits his knee."

"I should think he'd rather play golf."

"What you really mean by that, is that *you* would rather play golf."

My father-in-law's big living room is not only a living room in the orthodox meaning, but a hatching place for the cocoons of lunar moths and other *Lepidoptera*. The *Hymenoptera* are represented by one or more glass-cased anthills—over near the window by the grand piano, where he plays Bach fugues. The architect who built this window, and all other windows on that side of the house, is said to have suffered horribly. The windows are of thick plate glass, some of them almost six feet square.

"But you simply *can't* have windows like that in an English brick house!" the architect protested.

"Why can't you?" my father-in-law asked.

"It isn't *done!*"

"Well, it's time someone began. I'll be damned if

I'm going to cut up a good twenty-mile view with those little, leaded, window panes."

On a brisk Sunday afternoon in March or early April, you are likely to find him on the terrace flying a kite from a thousand-yard reel of twelve-thread cuttyhunk. At first you will think it odd that a man of sixty should engage in this childish practice. After a few moments, however, you will probably hear yourself saying: "Let me hold her for a while, do you mind?"

But beware. If the line parts while you are present, whether or not you are holding it, you will not see my father-in-law again until he has tracked down the kite. In that respect, he resembles a fox hound. If, as he disappears into the brush, he turns and shouts: "Want to come along?" you had better say "No, thanks," unless you are in excellent physical shape. Once a favorite kite came to earth in Henry Ford's peach orchard, and the retrieve called for a gruelling four-mile marathon.

People who fail to discriminate between manners and mannerisms probably think my father-in-law lacks dignity. But he is almost always dignified in the true sense, birch lice and all, whether receiving an honorary degree from a university, addressing an Economic Conference, reading a paper at Geneva, or spraying the fishing camp with Flit in his undershirt, the last thing before lights out.

He is one of the few people I know who are practically fearless. This makes his judgment in navigating northwest gales on the lake in a small boat very poisonous. But when you are with him in a squall you stop being frightened. It's like sailing with Captain Bligh.

Once he was scheduled to participate in a radio talk in Washington. Time was short, and the Bureau of Air Commerce sent up a Stinson and a pilot to ferry him to the Capital. I went along for the ride.

On the return trip we ran into fog. The left wing-tank was empty, and the right tank was very low. Static washed out the Newark-Boston beam, and I knew we were in a jam by the way the pilot batted his ear phones, trying to get a Boston weather report. All he got was a sound like someone breaking sticks in his ears. In the fog-dark, he lit a match now and then to check the dwindling gas supply.

Under those circumstances, you have a long, hurting fear—one that you can't walk away from. I stood it for an agonizing hour, and then put my mouth close to my father-in-law's ear and shouted: "Well, what do you think about *this?*" He did not deny that he was disturbed, but the main reason seemed to be that it had got dark at a moment when he had practically mastered a cross-word puzzle! "Only about three words to go," he grumbled.

Last January I almost went to Europe with my father-in-law. Heaven knows what would have happened if the trip had actually come off. Probably we would have fetched up against a brick wall in Madrid, father protesting in Spanish that he didn't want any darn bandage over his eyes, just go ahead and shoot. The trip was cancelled because he was taken ill in Washington and ordered to lie flat on his back for six weeks in the Emergency Hospital. The result was almost as bad.

When his son, J., and I, went down to Washington to see him, we were not greeted with the groans of the gravely ill, but with the following: "Your first assignment—some little bananas."

We demanded the reason why. It seems that J. had sent him some birch twigs and a juniper frond in a flower pot to cheer him with thoughts of brush-cutting with axe and bush-hook when he recovered. Doctors, orderlies and nurses had never laid eyes on such a quaint floral display, and had inquired as to its identity. Rather than go into an involved explanation, my father-in-law had told them it was a rare kind of banana tree, found only on the lower slopes of New England.

So J. and I deployed over the town to cover the assignment. We found the fruit bazaars of Washington devoid of little bananas, and we made several enemies during the search. Fruit vendors do not take kindly to you when you sidle up to them and say: "Have you any little bananas?" They want to know *why* you want them, and why regular bananas won't do. In order to shorten our explanation and make it sound plausible, we told one fruit dealer that we had a dear friend who had *bananaphobia*. It was a form of lunacy which could be cured only by a hot poultice of a bunch of dwarf bananas. The fruit dealer said that *we* were the crazy people, and not to come any nearer.

Finally we found an imaginative taxi driver, who entered into the spirit of the thing. He drove us to the market district. There, in a dank, tarantula-infested dungeon, we located two bunches of lethal-looking bananas about two inches long. We returned in triumph to the hospital, and by means of invisible threads, attached the bananas to the birch twigs, and all around in the sixth floor corridors you could hear the dark-skinned orderlies whispering: "That bush in 605 got *bananas* on it!"

There are certain Maine guides who were astonished to hear that my father-in-law lay still in a hospital for six weeks. "*Him!* By God, it ain't possible!"

[xviii]

Father always still-hunted alone, paddled his own canoe, and lugged at least one end of it on the carries. He has impressed his children, his children-in-law, and indirectly his grandchildren with the satisfaction which comes from doing one's full share on canoe trips. Thus we have all learned the ache of a heavy pack, and the feel of a canoe thwart on the backs of our several necks. And thus each expedition in the wild lands has its finest *esprit de corps* when he is along and running things.

I know no man who so thoroughly understands the idea of wilderness; no man so happily involved in its storms, its solitude, its beauty and its peace. I marvel at the sinew and flexibility of his mind; at his abiding sense of obligation to society; and at his comprehensive, unacademic knowledge of art, philosophy, music, science and mathematics.

On the same high plane on which he might inquire into the nature of scalar analysis, he has personally sampled the liver of a fresh salmon to determine whether it is palatable to man. He pronounced the salmon liver wanting, but porcupine livers are standard diet when available. It was only last June that, on Horseshoe Cove beach on Dobsis Lake, he took a pioneering bite of raw, washed-up smelt, and gave a gourmet's description of its taste while the rest of us stood around, grimacing. "A *little* bit too fishy," he proclaimed, smacking his lips; "but not unlike a herring I once ate in—in—Poland, I think it was."

It is impossible to know such a man long without thinking a great deal of him, and thinking of him a great deal. Therefore fragments of him appear in this volume, stivering along between the lines of "Lo, the Long Brown Ridges," "The Old Men Look Back," and again in the essential spirit of "The Tenderfoot Who Wasn't." Not only did my father-in-law introduce me to most of these adventures. He first taught me to cast a fly, and first told me to write, and he continues to set a fast pace at both. I cannot accurately estimate whether these tales are the flower of Henry S. Dennison's influence—or merely a fungus. But I dedicate them to him, just the same!

E.W.S.

Northampton, Mass., 1937.

A TOMATO CAN CHRONICLE
AND OTHER STORIES OF
FISHING & SHOOTING

A TOMATO CAN CHRONICLE

ONCE, our family lived at the end of a dusty road in a town which slept in winter and drowsed in summer. I remember splitting kindling on cold mornings. I remember the sound of the iron pump handle—its "ga-dunk, ga-dunk, ga-dunk." Early in the morning Mother used to come in and simply whip the bedclothes off my brother and me. We had the choice of getting up instanter, or lying there and freezing. In those days we ate in the kitchen, which is the best of all places to eat. You can hear the bacon sizzling, and see the golden nether side of the hot cake when the "flipper" lifts an edge. I remember fishing Neyhart's pond with Digsy Jones in Spring; and the sayings of Old Man Cartright who, I think, wanted nothing that he did not have. And one morning in particular—

The smoke from little chimneys climbed slowly. Hens clucked, and you could see robins flying with bits of old string in their beaks. It was one of those mornings when turtles gather on logs at the edge of the pond. It was June. It was still, yet it seemed as though you could hear things growing. School was just over. I was ten. That was a long, long time ago—and I sometimes wish it were today.

On the way home I took off my shoes and stockings, and under my feet the grass felt cool. Snedecker's wagon went by, leaving a sweet wake of pipe smoke, horse, and the first dust of Spring. The sun warmed my shoulder blades. A redwing blackbird sang wonderfully from his perch on a cattail in the swamp. I felt a great, brooding happiness—and both wonder and gladness at being alive, and free.

When I got home I found my mother sweeping. I never remember her doing nothing. Looking at her, I felt that she could not understand the bigness of my thoughts and my sensations. She glanced up at me—a quick, straight look of estimate. "Stand off the rug, Sonny. I want to take it up."

I stood off, surer than ever that I was a misunderstood and suffering boy. "Mother," I said, sadly, "have you got an old tomato can?"

"What for?"

"Worms."

"Have you cleaned up the cellar yet?" she asked, and I felt prickly with rebellion.

"Tomorrow, Mother. I'll clean it all up tomorrow."

"What's the matter with right now, dear?"

"Well—," I said, and looked out the window, where an oriole was fixing a nest in the droopy elm. Mother came and stood beside me and looked out, too. I know—now—that the look and sense of Spring were as wonderful to her as to me. She probably knew more about the way I felt than I did. She watched the oriole a second, and said: "There's a tomato can in the box under the sink. Careful not to cut yourself on the cover."

Ten minutes later Digsy Jones and I were in Digsy's barnyard with a spade and the tomato can. "I'll dig," I said, "and you pick 'em out. Put some dirt in for them to eat."

I turned a damp sod and demolished it, and there were no worms. I turned another, and another, and finally one which fairly bristled with pink fat ones. "Gosh a'mighty!" Digsy cried. "You struck a vein, Ed!"

I rapped the "pay sod" with the spade and hit Digsy's hand by mistake. "I'm awful sorry, Digsy. I never meant to."

"It don't hurt. Dig up another."

Presently we were away to Neyhart's pond. Barefooted, we kicked at the dust. Digsy was whistling. The tomato can was tucked inside my shirt, cold against my stomach. Our cane poles bobbed up and down, just out of synchrony with our steps, and the coarse line spooled 'round and 'round the tips reminded me of small hornets' nests in shape. Now and then our sinkers, a couple of nuts off an old stove bolt, would tap against our poles.

There is a curious wistfulness which pervades the spirits of barefoot boys in Spring. Perhaps already there's a hint that life is not as big as hope, or quite as sweet as memory. Yet it is a time and an age when gratification and yearning come close to balancing, which makes it difficult to explain unrest. Digsy expressed his by saying: "I wisht I could spit like Old Man Cartright."

"You can whistle better," I said.

"You can fish better than him, too," Digsy said.

Since Old Man Cartright had introduced us both to fishing, I was guilty of a kind of disloyalty when I replied: "It's how I bait up. Old Man Cartright doesn't leave any hanging. He had ought to leave three or four strands of worms dangling."

Digsy nodded, and for a time we shared one another's greatness in silence.

We walked out on the gray ledge that shelved into the pond, and I can remember the warmth of the granite on the soles of my bare feet. The water was deep here, and the shafts of sunlight would attract your eyes, and you'd follow them down and down, but you couldn't see bottom. I set the tomato can in a crevice

in the ledge, and we unwound our lines from the tips of the poles.

"How far you goin' to set your bobber?" Digsy asked.

I made a considerable pretense of studying "conditions" before I answered: " 'Bout five feet, I should say."

Digsy measured his line against mine, sliding his cork stopper up until it was even. Then he stuck his hand in the tomato can and drew out a worm. I did likewise. We baited up, spit hastily, and threw out. Then we sat on the ledge, elbows on knees, hands locked under our poles, the butts under us.

I looked furtively at Digsy's cork float, then at mine. He looked at mine, then at his, then at me. Each thought the other would get the first bite. A turtle poked a cautious triangular head above the surface, floated a while, and silently disappeared. The lily pads were up, the willows leafed out along shore. A flock of pigeons circled over Snedecker's barn, and about that time Digsy yanked, and a nine-inch yellow perch described an accurate arc, landing behind us in the alders.

Digsy's pole clattered on the ledge, and he ran back to pounce on the perch. Then my float bounced up and down and disappeared, and I had one. We laid them side by side on the ledge. "Mine's the big one," Digsy said.

I nodded: "Yuh, but they're almost the same."
"Almost."
"But not quite, Digsy. Yours is fatter."
Without another word, Digsy took a piece of licorice from his pocket and handed it to me for a bite. Then we threw out again. A dragon fly whizzed by, and you could see the sun on its wings. We used to call them devil's darning needles, and this one came so close that Digsy ducked his head.
"They won't sew your mouth up, Digsy," I said. "It's just a fib."
"Yes, they will," Digsy insisted. "Old Man Cartright said they would. He knows a boy that got sewed up by one, one time. They had to cut the stitches out."
Digsy was preparing further authentication of this surgical fable, when our corks plopped under the surface simultaneously. We stared, our eyes big, as the floats wobbled along a few inches under water, towed by we knew not what. This time when we yanked, Digsy had a big bluegill, and I had nothing but the remembered sensation of something heavy.
"You got to let them run longer before you yank," Digsy said, unhooking his bluegill.
"It was a bass," I mourned. "I just know it was a big bass."
"Try him again before he swims away," Digsy advised.

[6]

A castle of cloud climbed white above the fringe of maples and willows on the far shore. The pond was quiet, smooth, a mirror. We could look down and see our reflections, and—when we spit—they'd tremble and go to pieces. Digsy stuck his toes in the water and wiggled them. "It ain't warm enough yet," he said, significantly, but it made me want to go swimming just to hear Digsy's voice.

When I looked for my float, it had disappeared, and my line extended straight out toward the middle of the pond. I waited as long as patience itself, and then yanked. But when I yanked the fish didn't come up! I could feel him tugging and surging, and I felt weak with excitement. Digsy's eyes widened as he watched the tip of my pole whipping up and down. "He's gritting his teeth on it!" Digsy whooped, and it felt that way.

"Help me Digsy!" I yelled.

Digsy got a hold on the pole, and we strained upward, and it was a bass! He slithered all over the ledge, and we scrambled for him on our hands and knees, and whacked our heads together, but finally we got him down and kneeled on him. I suppose he weighed about three pounds, but to us he was an armful. Digsy hit him twice with a maple stick, and we stood on the ledge panting, talking and dancing with triumph.

Then Digsy borrowed my knife and went to cut a

crotch to string our fish on. I heard him say "Ouch!" and when he returned with the forked stick his left thumb was bleeding.

"Cut you, Digsy?" I said, very solicitously.

Digsy shrugged. "It's nothing," he said. "Just a flesh wound."

We started home, and I remember looking back just once at Neyhart's pond. Recently I saw the pond again—for the first time in over thirty years. It was exactly as it always was—except for three white swans, moving majestically on the surface. But I wonder what became of Digsy Jones? Someone said he was driving a grocery truck, and someone said he had moved away, but no one really knew. And I wonder about Old Man Cartright who showed us how to bait a hook, who smelled faintly of corncob pipe and beer, and who said: "Fishin' is when you ain't got no worry, nor no enemy, nor no dislike for nothin' nor nobody—an' they're bitin' good." Maybe Old Man Cartright was Huckleberry Finn!

THE TENDERFOOT WHO WASN'T

As soon as they got off the train at the flag station, Mercer began to deride the place, its dilapidation, even its unknown inhabitants. But Mr. Reuben Usher, who at sixty had never been in the wilderness, said quietly: "The stillness doesn't frighten me. I like it."

"You wait, Reuben," Mercer said. "The real stillness is when we get in the canoe—on the lake."

"And if it were noise I liked, then would you also know where were even finer noises?" said the old man, in a most patient voice.

"Humph," growled Mercer. "Like to zoom this dump in a plane. Bet they've never even heard one."

"Isn't there a Forest Service plane?"

"No." Mercer chuckled in his thought of startling the natives. Strident in the belief that he was a sportsman, he wore a heavily checked shirt, an exaggerated belt, and high laced boots. He was fat, bluff, permeated with his own heartiness. But on the splintered platform of the flag station, his uniform looked fake.

"Seems good to get the old woods clothes on again," he said, flexing his huge arms. "I wish young Ireland would hurry up. I told him nine o'clock in the *morning*. But time means nothing to these backwoods guides."

Mr. Usher remembered that he had come here by promise of the very timelessness which Mercer now impugned. He was glad in this new and tranquil environment, even though he felt ill-equipped to comprehend it. He felt a trenchant yearning to know, and to participate; and he pointed to some swallows mustered on the telegraph wires, and said: "Look, isn't that a storm warning?" Somewhere he had read that the congregating of swallows foretold a storm, and this small knowledge would be his contribution.

"Doesn't mean a thing," said Mercer, glancing contemptuously at the sky. "Not a cloud. It's clouds that count."

"I must have been misinformed."

"Takes experience to read weather right, Reuben. Of course I've been at it a long time. Were you worried about the canoe trip on the lake?"

"Maybe—maybe I was thinking of that, deep down."

Mercer strode away along the platform, and the old man looked wonderingly at the forest. He discovered it to be both beautiful and melancholy, and he resented the railroad tracks which had cut through it. Precocious, incredible tracks! He reflected that only twelve hours ago he had been at peace in the roaring twilight of the North Station, Boston. He had felt at home, consoled, one of a myriad beings bustling under a roof. But here—he was not quite sure. He was fascinated, troubled, wary, and profoundly reverent.

He looked beyond the tracks at the slow uncoiling of the river. Somewhere in his immense talk, Mercer had mentioned a rapid named Slewgundy Heater. Mr. Usher looked up the river as far as he could see, then down, believing he might be rewarded with a glimpse of this savage-sounding place. But from one direction the river flowed deathlessly out of the forest, and in the other as deathlessly into it. He was refreshed by the supernal stillness of the river's flowing.

In front of a shack on a slope, a sequestered prophet chopped wood. The old fellow seemed vastly unannoyed with this work, and the blows of his axe belonged. Never had Reuben Usher heard the "chock" of an axe in a clearing, yet by some miracle the sound was familiar. The odors of spruce and woodsmoke made him tingle, and he wished slyly for the nostrils of a hound so that he might sniff, and isolate even finer ingredients.

Thinking reverently of the forest, Mr. Usher saw how little of its meaning books might convey. After sixty years he felt on the brink of a new and more beautiful kind of life. He understood people, the management of industry, toil in the cities of the world. He knew music, literature, and painting, and he felt that music alone might construe the talents of the river, the forest, and the sky.

Now from the telegraph wires, the swallows twittered and made brief nervous flights, reminding Mr. Usher of his newness here. Again came Mercer in his brown, emphatic boots. Mercer trod auspiciously, and was a prophet of weather.

"Here comes Ireland!" the big man said. "He'll do anything for me. I knew his father well."

The earnest ears of a horse showed on the skyline, then horse, wagon and man were visible on the dusty road. Mercer was stimulated by Ireland's approach. "Well, how do you like it, Reuben?"

"It's good," said Mr. Usher, softly.

"You'll catch on. Wait till you get on the lake and catch your first trout. Ever been in a canoe much?"

He had told Mercer several times that he knew nothing of canoes, but he repeated patiently: "Just once, in the park, when I was a boy."

Mercer chuckled as if his knowledge of canoes were occult and patented. "This is the real stuff." Then, lowering his voice in confidence, he said: "You ought to have bought high laced boots and woolen pants."

The old man looked gravely at his linen trousers, his new white sneakers, and his shaker sweater.

"Mark you as a tenderfoot right away," said Mercer, disapprovingly.

"I am a tenderfoot."

"Yes—but you don't want them to think so."

When the wagon drew up, Mercer gave the horse a dusty slap, and was first to greet Steve Ireland.

"Hello there, Stevie. Knew your old man well, so we'll start right off with first names, eh? Mine's Al. Al Mercer."

"Yes," Steve said. "I've heard of you Mr. Mercer."

"Brought my friend Usher—Reuben Usher. He's interested in a little rest in this country you fellows have got up here. How the trout biting?"

"Ought to pick up a few."

They climbed into the wagon and started toward the lake, and the wheel-sounds were muffled in the dust. Everywhere the sun shone on deserted fields, and on the leaves of Spring.

Mr. Usher noted that Steve was young, lank, and sinewy. He looked straight ahead, and listened calm-faced to Mercer's outbursts of lore. Steve was not uncommunicative. He was reserved, quietly and courteously withholding his personality, as if he felt too many men had tried to get acquainted with him in seconds. As they passed a farm, Steve looked long at an old cow which lay on the grass. He looked from the cow to the sky, then straight ahead again. "Cow layin' down in the mornin'," he said. "Storm 'fore night."

"Not today, Stevie," contradicted Mercer. "Not a cloud in the sky. I was telling Reuben, it's clouds that count."

Steve nodded, and Mr. Usher felt a deep affection for his swallows.

Before they reached the lake, a buck deer cleared the road ahead of them in a single leap. Astonished, Mr. Usher rose from his seat, as if with longing to capture and suspend this flash of beauty. For him all the forest was enriched by the live, wild thing which was a part of it.

At first sight of the deer, Steve's eyes had darkened in a quick and savage joy. Steve Ireland was a native hunter; and, crouched on the wagon seat, he had gestured fiercely, saying: "God! Look at him! Look! Look!" Then he sat back, sighing, relaxed, his lips wrinkling in a dreamful smile. Damp beech leaves on a long ridge, a fire no bigger than the bottom of a tea pail, liver broiling on a stick, and that buck hanging by his gambrels from a bent sapling. Peace and plenitude were Steve's. He wanted only things which were probable of fulfilment, and he did not wonder whither he was going, or why. Here was this buck, working in his country! He looked artlessly around him, saying in his mind: "I'll hunt this ridge, come fall. I'll dump that critter on his nose before a lynx gets him. Gawd A'mighty, I can taste the gravy now, and the drool a-gatherin' in my mouth a'ready."

"Lot of deer up around Jackman," Mercer informed. "That's the place to see deer. Ever up around Jackman, Stevie?"

"No."

"You ought to try it there some time."

Through the trees the lake shone with abrupt radiance, like daylight at the end of a tunnel. Mr. Usher climbed from the wagon, and walked with boyish eagerness to the sand beach. He stood there, a silver sheen of hair curling from under his hat. He felt strangely beholden to something. He could not remember when he had felt both awe and gratitude simultaneously. Was it the long mystery of distance? The remote and dusky shores? The boulders atop themselves in trembling mirage? Or was it simply the hovering paternity of earth and sky? Oh, he would bring his children here, and show this to them, watching while it penetrated them as it penetrated him.

Beneath a dignified spruce, Mercer babbled and assembled fly rods. Steve unhooked, and hung the harness on a tall gray stump. He waved to the horse, and said: "Go it, old Crawnch! Go it, boy!" The horse shook, and trotted up the road, its destination private.

At the edge of the forest, Steve rolled a green canoe to his shoulder and brought it down to the beach. He thrust the bow into the water, loaded the duffel, and took a long steady look into the northwest.

"How far is it to camp?" asked Mr. Usher.

"They call it eleven miles. I guess we're all set, sir." Steve leaned on his paddle, and while he waited, stared again at the sky. The cloud was there, all right—black, and low down in the horizon.

Mr. Usher stooped and touched the gunwale of the canoe. "This is all new to me, you know," he said.

Mercer, having finished with the rods, came down in time to overhear this. "Don't worry, Reuben. A canoe'll scare you to death before it'll drown you. Right, Stevie?"

Steve nodded toward the bow, and said to Mercer: "Will you sit forward, please?"

Mercer stepped in and moved to his position. "That's a fact, though—about canoes, isn't it Stevie?"

Steve's active eyes squinted a trifle as they focussed for an instant on the low-lying cloud. "That's what they say," he said. Bending, he steadied the canoe for Mr. Usher. "Just step in the middle of her. Here, grab my shoulder. And when you set down, rest your back agin the middle thwart an' face towards me."

Carefully the old man did as he was told, and he marvelled at the grace with which Steve shoved off and jumped into the stern, his moccasins making scarcely a whisper on the cedar planking of the craft. Steve's paddle knifed into the water, and the canoe moved out into the lake.

Mr. Usher peered into the water. The sides of boulders loomed, fell away to depth and darkness. Mercer had begun casting, and was making handsome predictions as to the size and number of trout he would take. But it appeared that his prophecies were delayed of fulfilment, and he grew petulant and dismayed, and spoke of great catches in Moosehead Lake, and of rainbows from the Cowichan River on Vancouver Island, and of the merits of many places quite impossible to reach at the moment.

"Why don't you get the canoe out farther?" he said to Steve. "Can't you tell by this time they're not lying in close?"

"Just as you say," said Steve. He had been following the margin of an underwater bar, but he nosed the canoe outward. For a while they fished fruitlessly a quarter mile off shore, and Mercer began again: "This is too far out. I didn't mean this far. Can't you take us where they are?"

Steve angled toward shore until he picked up the shadowy outline of the bar again. It was his job to keep his sportsmen happy, and to do what they said, no matter what. It was also his job to keep an eye on the cloud which stretched long and straight across the northwest. Maybe it was just as well their backs were turned to this cloud. He rolled a cigarette, and had trouble making the paper stick. "I got the driest spit of any man I ever see," he finally remarked, tossing the cigarette away.

In the narrows between two long points, Mercer began to catch trout. He grew voluble, informative, and obstreperously happy. "See? I told you, Reuben," he chimed. Everything he said was loud and definite, and his voice re-echoed from the point. Mr. Usher felt curiously glad of this double stating. The stillness was now hovering, oppressive, and Mercer's prattling somehow served as a contact with humanity.

"Got another!" he shouted. "A beauty. Say, how many I got now all together?"

"You got enough," said Steve. "Shall I let this one go?" Paddle balanced across his knees, Steve held the trout underwater in the net.

"Let it go?" protested Mercer. "What's the sense in catching them if you let them go?"

"He'll live. You got more'n you can eat a'ready."

"Let him go," said Mr. Usher.

A few moments later, Mr. Usher felt a violent tug on his line. He had been trying to cast, and, doing rather badly, had allowed his fly to trail in the water. As the trout struck, he had instinctively lifted his tip and hooked the fish. He sat forward, eyes sparkling with delight, his lips spread in an embarrassed smile.

"Steve! What shall I do now?"

"Reel in! Reel in!" interrupted the tireless Mercer. "Keep a taut line! How do you like it now, Reuben?"

"You're doin' all right, Mr. Usher," Steve said, peering into the water. "Good fish. Go mighty near two pound."

Suddenly the old man's line went slack, and the spring of the rod whipped the fly clear of the surface.

"Gone! But I don't care, Steve—not if you don't. Really."

Steve grinned at him, and Mercer said: "What did I say about keeping a taut line? You can't catch trout unless you learn the art of keeping a taut line. Right, Steve?"

"Well, it's too bad Mr. Usher," Steve said. "Your first one, too."

"But I'm just as happy. Really, I've never been so happy."

Steve had no time to savor his wish that all men were like Mr. Usher. A puff of wind snapped out of the northwest, and a dark cat's paw rushed across the water. The wind reached them all in a cold, quick pressure which put Steve's hatbrim flat against his forehead, and brought the water to his eyes. His lips twitched and tightened as he reached for his hat. He was looking far away at the cloud, and he saw that its lower edge was ripped and lacy.

The canoe emerged between the two points into the widening body of the lake. Distances stretched ahead, and to the right and left. Steve looked measuringly at Cardiff Point. He could duck behind it if things got bad. Or, if the sportsmen wanted to reach camp, he might try for the lee of Munson Island, three miles away. His two passengers sat with their backs to the cloud, and they had not seen it. When the time was right, he would call it to their attention. Anticipating that moment, he gave them both a sharp glance of estimate. Steve had classified them simply as the fat bastard in the bow, and the old man aft of the middle thwart. You could feel the wind pretty good now, he thought—a cold one. The lake was rippling some, too, and the spruce tops waving on Cardiff Point. . . .

Mr. Reuben Usher reeled in his line, and sat thinking, his eyes half closed. The young guide, so close to him in the stern of the eighteen-footer, had a quality which he hoped his own sons might some day possess. This quality, Mr. Usher believed, concerned the patience to remove ten thousand stones from a field, and the reticence to hew in a clearing. What if one transplanted himself permanently into this environment? What would he miss first? One wanted to cry out: "I would miss nothing!" But was that true? Mightn't one long for good music, for his work, or for someone with whom to draw comparisons?

An unfamiliar rocking of the canoe disturbed him. Glancing about, he noted some remarkable changes. Everywhere was motion. The waves marched in sharp, unending echelons, and trees swayed against the sky. In any direction it was a long way to shore, but you could see the swaying of trees, distance or no! Young Steve had changed his course, so that he quartered into the waves. These waves slapped briskly against the starboard bow, and they seemed impious, and direly purposeful.

Down wind came an eerie babel of laughter, and Mr. Usher thought suddenly of ghouls, and glanced apprehensively at Steve.

"Loons," Steve said, serenely. "They do that sometimes when the weather's changing." He stuck his hand in the water and scooped some to his mouth. Wiping his lips, he said: "Better reel in now, Mr. Mercer."

"Reel in? Why should I reel in?" the big man queried.

Steve twitched his paddle. The canoe swung sharply, rolling in the trough of the waves. At this angle, by turning their heads slightly, all three men could see the cloud. Its forward edge was smooth, dense, jet black; and its trailing edge was torn and coppery.

"See that?"

Mr. Usher nodded. His swallows! They had been right!

"Well, what about it?" Mercer asked.

"Wind."

"So what? What's a little wind?"

Mr. Usher observed that the men were shouting, not in anger, but to make themselves heard. The wind pressed hard upon his cheek and howled in his head. He had read of squalls, but there must be a limit, a restriction somewhere on velocity. At a certain point in the wind's acceleration, it ceased its benediction, and became arrogant, menacing, and cold. It knocked the tops from selected waves, and scattered them on the back of one's neck.

"I can make Cardiff Point," yelled Steve, his shirt ballooning, "or I can try for Munson Island. Camp's on the mainland, just beyond Munson. What do you want to do?"

"It'll blow over," said Mercer, reeling in. "You're not scared of a little wind, are you Stevie? Head for Munson Island."

Steve snatched off his hat, placing it on the floor of the canoe, his knee on the brim. The wind tussled his black hair, parting it indiscriminately and showing the white scalp. "Suit yourself," he said.

The cloud shut off the sun, and the sun's abatement

did something ominous to the scenery and to the moods of the men. In the dim light the waves became black and murderous, and their crests hissed, and were dirty white. Steve began to study them steadily, and not just once in a while.

Mr. Usher wished they were now about to land on Munson Island; but Munson was an imperishably far distance, and this was so of all shores, and the canoe seemed to be making no headway. He recalled two recent shouts from Mercer, and in these shouts he perceived a special significance which he had not noticed at the time.

One shout had been: "How do you like it now, Reuben?" and this had been in a kind of paper-thin voice, a voice uncertain of itself. The second shout had been directed to Steve: "Why don't you turn and run with it—*any* shore?"

"Swamp over the stern," Steve had answered.

Thereafter, Mercer had been silent, and Mr. Usher realized that Mercer was frightened, and that he himself was frightened, and that of all living men, Steven Ireland was most important. There was something very illogical about their predicament. You could step away from an onrushing train, a tiger, or a madman. But you could not step away from this.

Always Mr. Usher had regarded wind as something wild, free, and magnificent. He saw now that it was also wanton, merciless, and unpredictable. It snapped off the top of any tree at random. It filled the air with frayed leaves, and tumbled crows in their stride. Moreover, it imparted to the lake a cold, coherent lust.

The waves came close and crowding. They came on, towering, toppling, threatening Steve Ireland's precocious vigilance. And the waves applauded themselves by the hiss of their torn crests.

The canoe lurched, and a gout of spray spilled over them, spanked the bottom of the canoe, and cascaded toward the stern. Steve steadied her with his knees, and yelled to Mercer: "Lay down! Lay down! They don't get no smaller if you rise up an' look at 'em. I said lay *down!*"

Mr. Usher's stolen glances toward Munson Island brought nothing but a sickening sight of power beyond belief. They would never make it! And if there were no progress, why continue this teetering, this hypocritical effort to keep the bow of a canoe in one direction? Munson Island was a bait designed by experts in irony. It was a thing toward which to struggle in vain. They had all been very cunningly trapped!

The old man felt that his fear was degrading and shameful; and he wondered how long a human being could live in its concentrated misery. Many times in life he had been startled, momentarily filled with terror. Time was the element which differentiated between fear and a mere fright. Mr. Usher knew that his wish to pray was weak and pitiful, because he knew it was merely the wish to live. But he said in his mind:

"God, please wait a minute if You can. God, what is a minute to You?" He knew it was his finest prayer.

He was wet clear through, and when the canoe heaved under him, he seemed to compress, growing inferior in stature and great in circumference. Whereupon, the canoe pitching downward over a crest, he became a being of only vertical dimension, and all his width was evaporated. He could anticipate these mad sequences by the crackling antagonism in Steve's eyes. Steven Ireland knew exactly how to look at a wave, and the look was not scornful.

The old man began arranging sincere objections to his own drowning. There was too much work left undone. A man should be duly warned and prepared for such a climax as his own death. He should be permitted to order his larger work of life, so that it could be entrusted to an able successor. But it didn't work out that way. Had he actually believed that he would lie down some day in a quiet place and say: "Now I am ready to die"? If so, he had been guilty of false thinking, for it was apparent that one could prepare only for life. In fact much of life was nothing else. Death had its own incalculable volition, and anyone who thought it might procrastinate in his favor was a fool.

Munson Island was undoubtedly a beautiful place where men could walk, or lean gratefully against trees and stare out at this cold compendium of hell.

Mercer, who had been so boisterous, so ebullient in the placid wilderness, lay in the bow, eyes shut, face slack and ugly in his terror.

Steven Ireland knelt in the stern, working. Mr. Usher believed him possessed of all knowledge useful on earth, as well as an amazing sense of balance. Steve must also have an unswerving egotism to engage these waves. His hair was whipped and stringy with spray. Water dripped from him and was blown to vapor. When Mercer moved, a victim of his own panic, Steve yelled: "Lay down!" He yelled so that the cords in his neck strung tight, but his voice was reduced to a whisper in the howl of wind and crashing of the seas.

Without realizing what had happened to him, Mr. Usher had buried his fear in his admiration for Steve. The situation itself belonged to Steven Ireland. He alone was useful and articulate. His patience was an enduring attribute, proof against this wave, the next, and all others. Steve was here against his own judgment, the only judgment which counted. But he wasted no time in thinking he would soon be dead. He did not appear enraged at anyone for getting him into this, yet each paddlestroke must have drawn achingly of his strength. His shirt was a wet skin plastered over his

chest. Under it the muscles showed lean and live. He was incurably busy. No sooner would he defeat one wave, than he would be about the outrageous problem of the next. He took no time for triumph, breathing, or oration.

Of a sudden Mr. Reuben Usher came aware of his own returning courage. Winning this fight no longer seemed grievously important—if only he could help Steve. The old man's eyes glowed with his unwieldy excitement. He leaned forward, crying out through his numbed mouth: "I want to help!"

Steve's lips curled briefly from his teeth. Without taking his eyes from the waves, without missing a stroke, he reached behind him and tossed an empty lard pail into Mr. Usher's lap. *"Bail her!"*

Working joyfully with his lard can, Mr. Usher bailed. In time he developed a great pride in his technique. He found that he could plan his awkward scooping when the canoe was tipped, and thus get nearly a full pail at a scoop. On these great occasions, he would glance warily at Steve, and Steve was infallible and wordless in his gratitude. This moment, felt the old man, was very close to inspiration . . . when one fears nothing, when everything at once seems fine, and in one's heart is the wholesale evidence of truth.

At length they came exhausted into the lee of Munson Island, and now that rest and security were at hand, they doubted the violence of their own adventure. No one, they felt, could have come through alive. They must have been imagining things. But on the mainland, less than half a mile distant, they saw a cluster of motionless men. Then they had had witnesses! Then it was true! Steve wigwagged with his paddle, and all the men on the mainland waved their arms at once, and moved about in a state of excitement.

Steve sided the canoe into a sheltered cove on the island, and held her steady while Mr. Usher stepped out. The old man's legs were cramped and stiff. They buckled beneath him, and he felt himself obliged to fall down. The stones upon which he lay seemed to heave, as if the waves had imparted a habit to them. Steve Ireland bent over him and lent him a hand.

"Mine won't straighten out neither," the boy said. "It's like they're wore away to a couple of danglin' cords, ain't it?"

Steve got his axe from the stern and walked off looking for a dry pine stub. When he had gone, Mercer raised his head and looked around, blinking. Mercer did not disembark from the canoe. Rather, he emerged from it, like some huge and lumpish animal. At the sound of an axe, he glanced along the beach, noting that Steve was well out of earshot.

"That was awful, Reuben," he began.

Mr. Usher scarcely heard, so intent was he upon

the nearness of trees, and upon the feel of round stones and earth.

Mercer was regaining confidence and voice. "That was some blow, Reuben. Ireland had no business getting us into that, you know. It's sheer luck we weren't all drowned."

Reluctantly Mr. Usher turned his gaze away from some flies which by a method known only to themselves had congregated in numbers on the calm water.

"What did you say?" the old man asked.

Mercer began to pace the beach, to gesticulate. "I say that young fool has poor judgment. I'm going to see to it that his guide's license is revoked permanently."

"Oh, do they have to have licenses?"

"Licenses? Certainly. Take his license away, and he can't guide, see? Teach him a lesson."

Mr. Usher reached into his shirt pocket for a cigar. Sorrowfully he discovered that his supply had become a dark brown mush, which had stained his shirt. He turned his head slightly, noting that Steve had a fire started between two boulders up the shore. Woodsmoke! The old man's nostrils twitched, and in him there awakened strange longings.

"My fortune is considerable," he said, very soberly. "And I had wished to divide it equally among my sons. But if you should happen to have that boy's license revoked, I shall gladly spend the whole fortune reinstating it."

"You're crazy, Reuben. You don't understand."

The old man stood up and walked to the fire which was blazing merrily. Steve knelt close beside it, drying his clothes, and melting the chill from his bones. As Mr. Usher approached, Steve jumped up and handed him an ancient coat, resplendent with elbow patches and assorted buttons.

"By God," he said, evenly, "you put this on."

Mr. Usher did as he was bid, and pointed curiously to Steve's feet. "Do you suppose you could get me a pair of moccasins exactly like yours, Steve?"

"Why, sure. Sheldeye Linton makes them, by the old Britton tan. I give a dollar an' thirty-five for these."

Mr. Usher licked his lips. He leaned against the side of a boulder and stared into the fire. "Was it really a bad blow, Steven?"

"It was real bad."

"Well—tell me this: when you see a lot of swallows together, is that a sign of a storm?"

Steve nodded affirmatively and dropped a piece of split cedar on the fire. The old man smiled, as if he knew his next question were to be boyish, as if he could not resist asking it.

"Was I any use to you—out there?"

Steve pushed his hat back on his head. He lowered his voice the merest trifle, then bent closer over the fire.

"I wisht they was all like you," he said. "Jesus, I do!"

LOST: TWO REPUTATIONS

THE Canadian press, like Canadian rivers, is exceedingly cordial to visiting fishermen—and their wives. My first trip to the Nepisiquit River in northern New Brunswick was deemed worthy an item in the *Northwoods Axeman*, weekly. Mr. and Mrs. Oliver H. P. Rodman were my companions in the adventure, and even a casual reading of the news item establishes the fact that Mrs. Rodman, hereinafter known as Doro, attracted the spotlight to us.

Gloomily I quote from the *Northwoods Axeman*, issue of July 22, 1933: "Mr. and Mrs. Oliver H. P. Rodman, and Mr. Edmund Ware Smith, all of Massachusetts, U.S.A., have been fishing the Nepisiquit River this week. Mrs. Rodman, an attractive brunette, caught a brook trout of four and one-half pounds, as well as several of about four pounds. Mr. Rodman and Mr. Smith also fished."

How we "also fished" is described with fidelity, detail, and minimum acrimony in the following narra-

tive which, like all true confessions, begins with a quotation from a diary, thus:

JULY 14TH: OLLIE, DORO, AND I BOARD BOAT FOR
ST. JOHN, N.B. MY FIRST FISHING TRIP IN COM-
PANY WITH LADY. APPREHENSIVE!

We leaned on the after rail of the six-thousand-ton
coast liner, *S.S. St. John*, and sighed with that curiously exalted relief which comes of work done, play
begun—and the destination a strange river six hundred
miles to the north. I felt a sudden affection for this
little steamer. Outward bound, she was our transport
to freedom, our ferry to some of the finest squaretail
trout fishing in North America. And homeward bound,
she seemed to respect the melancholy of journey's end.

Sundown: No land in sight, and we quartered into a
heavy swell. The sky, the sea, the following gulls—all
were abruptly swallowed in a Bay of Fundy fog. We
could hear the monotonous "*o-o-o-o-o-m*" of the fog
horn at forty-second intervals; and away to starboard
the answering "o-o-o-o-o-m" of a ghost-ship asking
to pass in the night.

From a dance-floor on A-deck a good orchestra had
begun to play "Stormy Weather". It was cold outside,
and we went into the Beverage Room, contrasting its
luxury with tomorrow's imagined wilderness. Traditionally, a place where drinks are served is called a bar.

But the people who sponsored the *S.S. St. John* must have revolted under the shackles of custom. They called it Beverage Room, and there we sat in red leather chairs sipping Scotch and water, and discussing rivers, trout, and probable weather. There was a particular scrap of dialogue which bears like the stern of a hornet on subsequent events. Ollie and I were speculating as to whether it was more fun to fish with one fly or two on a leader, when Doro interrupted our weighty discourse by saying, dreamily: "I wonder who'll catch the largest trout."

From such a speculation comes only misery. It is the sort of thing that ladies should not be allowed to wonder about. And I hold that even men should wonder about it only in the dead of night when they are alone in bed. Courteously I assured Doro that she herself would catch this superlative fish, adding that the important thing was not size or numbers, but *how*. Her husband also awarded Doro the likelihood that she would take the biggest—but both he and I felt secretly that we were lying.

Under date of July 15th, my diary says:

GOT CAR OFF BOAT AND DROVE TO BATHURST, N.B.

That threadbare entry is a howling injustice to a tireless spruce forest; to fifty rivers, big and little; to glimpsed bits of blue sea, such as Shediac Bay where

Balbo's Italian invincibles wet their pontoons on their six-thousand-mile flight from Rome to Chicago; to the forty-mile road hewn through the forest from Chatham to Bathurst, on which you are likely to meet no more than one car, one wagon, one bicycle, one cow, one goat; to the neat signs which, spelled perpendicularly, announce the names of tiny wood-burning towns; to the inspired absence of bill boards; to conversation with natives in rusty French; and, lastly, to the town of Bathurst, where a man may still see sparks flying in a blacksmith's shop and English sparrows feasting happily in the street. Diaries are too succinct. The next entry is:

Went Up River That Night

The Bathurst Hunting & Fishing Lodges are four picturesque peeled spruce cabins twelve miles apart on the Nepisiquit River. Number One cabin is thirty miles up, above Grand Falls. To get there, you drive from Bathurst five miles in a car to what is known as the "Y." The "Y" is the point where the Canadian National Ry. separates from and abandons for all time a railroad which is its exact opposite. The C.N. Ry. has called itself the longest railroad in the world. But the Bathurst & Lower Nepisiquit Seaboard Airline Ltd. is the shortest, and is otherwise unique in matters of cross-country navigation. It has sixteen and one-half miles of rails which were laid by a crew having independent ideas of direction. Here no dull, scientific precision, but instead a fine carefree road with a sort of here-a-rail, there-a-rail spirit prevailing.

The rolling stock consists of a pint-size flatcar with a tent pitched on it, a one-lunged gasoline engine, Mr. Link LeBritton at the throttle, and practically no brakes at all. We all climbed aboard of her and took firm hold. Link ignited his corncob pipe, opened the throttle wide, and leaned back for peace and contemplation. Concerning the railroad experience, the diary has just a word. The word is:

RABBITS

I am more than ever convinced that my diary is a paragon of understatement; for, from the "Y" to the abandoned iron mine above Grand Falls, is virtually an unending vista of rabbits. They haunt the road-bed in quest of salt. Of course there are a few jack pines and mountains en route, but the rabbits dominate in the end. Using the ties of the Bathurst & Lower Nepisiquit Seaboard Airline Ltd. to sit down on, they regard the onrushing flatcar with sedate unconcern, waiting until it is within three feet before deftly side-hopping into the bush.

Darkness dropped a black wing over the wilderness as we reached the deserted mine. We said good-bye to

Link LeBritton and nosed our three canoes into the sleepy current. In the stern of each canoe was a guide whose name we had heard, whose hand we had shook, but whose face we had not seen. A mile of meandering water, and old man Nepisiquit burst into song.

To start up an almost legendary river at night is a strange and beautiful experience. A night hawk who-o-omed in pursuit of some hapless insect. An owl hooted from the depths of the black forest. The river hissed in the unseen grasses of the shores. The sky burned with brilliant northern stars; and, as we crossed a quiet eddy, a heavy trout—oh, it *must* have been a trout!—broke the surface, swirled, and went down. My eyes bulged in the dark, and I felt near to whatever it is that makes the universe move.

Lloyd Black, my guide, shipped his paddle and pulled a shod canoe pole from under the thwarts. I heard the steel shoe click on the rocks of the river bottom, felt the canoe lunge forward as Lloyd leaned on the pole. I squirmed with that itching discomfort which comes when one man is doing alone the work which two may share.

"Got another pole?" I said.

"Sure," said Lloyd, and presently we were working together, and the sweat came on my forehead and trickled down my nose, and Lloyd and I were calling each other by our first names.

At ten o'clock we reached the Narrows cabin. It is situated on an eighty-foot bluff, where at night you can hear the river. But you can't see it! Where, if for six months you have been dreaming about that river, you stand with your heart thumping, and try to wipe away the dark; where you picture in your mind just how the water will look, the shape of the rocks and trees, the color of the sky; where you tremble with excitement, with hope, and with hunger for the light of day.

I have never been capable of unpacking my fishing tackle within an area much less than half an acre. In two minutes, Ollie and I had made of the cabin floor a dismaying litter of rods, reels, lines, flies, flies, flies, leader boxes, packs, rain shirts, and bottles of fly dope. We jointed our rods, and put leaders to soak. Every now and then, as if it were carefully rehearsed, we glanced at one another and silently stepped outside to listen to the river, and smell it. It sounded to us like the laughter of angels, and it smelled clean and cool as a lawn after a rain. But the night was drenched with the scent of damp spruce which is solely a wilderness odor. Above us, almost low enough to touch, hung the magic northern stars.

Back in the cabin, Doro was examining the contents of a fly box by lamplight. She selected a Royal Coachman, held it to the light, and asked if it were a Wickham's Fancy. Ollie grinned wanly. Then she picked up a Dark Montreal, and said: "I know the name of this one."

"You do? What is it?" Ollie asked.

"It's a Black Gnat!"

Lastly she selected a red and white feathered fly with a silver body and jungle-cock shoulders. Ollie winced, and before Doro had a chance to guess again, he said: "No it isn't! It's a Doctor Breck!"

"I knew it all the time," Doro said. "Why did you tell me? It's the fly I'm going to use first tomorrow."

"Why?" her husband asked.

"Because I knew the name of it."

In the light of coming events, I am not here justified in going into an ancient theme—the logic of womankind. It's a great cause, but a lost one. It will get you in the end, like death, and taxes, and the lone mosquito in the tent. But I am fairly obliged to say that Doro had poled bow in a twenty-foot canoe four miles that night; that she did not shudder when owls hooted; that she helped her guide, Jim Black, tote the duffel up the eighty-foot bluff in the dark; that when June bugs banged against the screen door she did not make Ollie go out and see if it were robbers; that it was her first trip north of Boylston and Tremont Streets, Boston; that, hang it all, she very definitely belonged!

Morning came with a blazing orange sunrise, and I took my first look at the river—just stood there gulping it in. Directly below me, Douglas Goode, and Lloyd and Jim Black had started a tiny birch fire. In the still air, the smoke climbed slowly up to mingle with the fir tops. The boys had heated the ring of an old boom chain, and were patching the canoes with marine glue. They harmonized perfectly with their surroundings, and they satisfied my conception of good guides and companions. Otherwise, they proved to be the most skilful rivermen of my experience.

The Nepisiquit flows east by northeast, emptying into the Bay Chaleur at Bathurst. Its average width is about sixty yards. Its water is clear as glass, its depth, except for pools, about two feet in normal water. Its banks are crowded with spruce, fir, white birch, and popple.

When you cast a fly in the waters of the Nepisiquit you are never sure whether a seven-incher or a three-pounder will rise. To the fly fisherman, this kind of uncertainty is sheer perfection. It gives him that taut, tingling suspense which puts an edge on the finest sport in the world. There are more and larger trout in the Nepisiquit than in any river I have fished. To my certain knowledge there is at least one trout which weighs seven pounds. I have seen him, touched him, hefted him, felt the power of him. So has Ollie. But wait!

Trout water! What is the point of a mortal trying to describe something which is timeless, which in color, sound, and form is ever changing? A river which has both voice and silence?

Late on the first day up river, Lloyd held the canoe on the edge of an eddy: boulder, leaning cedar, birch and jack pine in the background. There I straightened out my first business cast on the Nepisiquit River. One of Joe Messinger's Pink Lady fanwings drifted for five seconds below the boulder. *"Whack!"*

Ollie and Douglas Goode saw the trout take, and they let out a brace of full-toned war whoops. I netted the fish—twelve and one-half inches, an even pound. That's a fat and beautifully formed trout. Outside he was the color of a Wyoming sunset. Inside he was salmon pink and tasted, along with half a dozen others, like something they design exclusively for the residents of Olympus.

"Nice little trout," said Douglas.

I traded a glance with Ollie, and his face elongated.

"You mean they come bigger?" he asked Douglas.

"Yes—three or four times as big."

Before we reached the mouth of Lazor's Brook, I learned that this was no idle affirmative invented for an occasion.

Ollie made a careful cast in the lower reaches of Lazor's Brook pool. Directly beneath his yellow bucktail, it appeared that a washtub, with attendant commotion, had sunk.

"Never touched him!" cried Ollie, his eyes protruding.

"Rest him," I said. "Change flies and try him again, later."

We held our canoe in the clear as Ollie began again to work on the trout. The late sun gleamed along the length of his backcast, and his Montreal dropped nicely. Nothing doing. He tried a Greenwell's Glory, a Leadwing Coachman, and three different bucktails.

"You try," he said, shrugging.

"No," I said.

"Yes."

"All right."

At this precise moment, Jim Black and Doro hove into view. They poled leisurely, nosing into the bank now and then to admire the fireweed or star flowers along shore. As they neared the pool, I remember Doro saying that she wanted to straighten out her line. Unaware that we had a big one located, she shot a very creditable cast over the velvet water and began to reel in. Well—she straightened her line, all right. At least something did! I have never seen a straighter line, nor a more surprised cluster of males in the aggregate.

"Give him line!" "Don't give him line!" "Keep the tip up!" "Get him onto the reel!"

The center of a group of four frenzied gentlemen, Doro alone remained calm. Quietly, peremptorily, and with perfect dignity, she caught the trout. This was the fish referred to by the *Northwoods Axeman.* It weighed exactly four pounds and eight ounces on the spring scales. Its length is emblazoned on Jim Black's paddle blade by a notch which he cut twenty inches from the tip.

After the trout was safely in the canoe, we gathered around and explained to Doro all the things she had done wrong. I told her some things. Ollie told her some things. Lloyd and Douglas added a few laconic suggestions. But Jim Black, who was her guide, said: "Me, personal, I figure she done all right." Jim's philosophy, like that of Bliss Perry's immortal worm-fisherman, is one of results.

As she listened to our ranting, Doro's modestly downcast eyes regarded the fly which was attached to the end of her leader. It was the Doctor Breck!

How does a riverman recall his river? Why, by its rapids, its rocks, and its campsites, probably. There was Lazor's Brook cabin, where the great mosquito migration occurred; Indian Falls, where you sleep with the rapids' throaty thunder in your ears; and the Elbow, where the eating of the mysterious lost blend fish chowder took place; and Billy Gray's camp, where, carved on an old lumberman's tally stick, were these words: "Octubr 4, 1907, shot one carrybou today. All hans gut dronk. i gut dronk two time."

But the trout fisherman remembers his river by its pools: Gravelly Pool, where, on Joe Messinger's hallowed fanwings, I caught my two biggest trout of the trip; the Bear House Pool, where several trout rose and actually took tiny dry flies while they were still in the air. There was Indian Falls, where, in the lower pitch, Ollie took six beauties during a severe thunder storm, two weighing three pounds. And the Devil's Elbow Pool, where I fell in. And Doro Eddy, named for Mrs. Rodman when she caught a four pounder, and where, in his thirty-five years' experience on the Nepisiquit, Jim Black had never known of a trout being taken!

We had turned brown as Indians, and the black flies shunned us now, as being mere chunks of shoe leather or old scrap iron. Ollie and I fished industriously about six hours daily. Sheepishly we would nick a paddle blade for our largest fish each day—but along toward sundown, Doro would glide near a fishless pool, cast for half an hour, and come drifting into camp with another day's record.

I believe firmly that competition does not belong in fishing. But I was beginning to take it seriously, and so was Ollie. I can still hear Jim Black's delighted chortling. "You boys cast a very han'some fly," he'd say. "I ain't never seen han'somer. Heh-heh-heh."

And Doro would remonstrate with him: "Jim, you mustn't!"

The lady of the expedition catches the big trout one day, perhaps two, or even three days. Fine! You congratulate her with some show of honest feeling. But when she does it seven days hand-running, your words sound a little hollow, like someone muttering in an iron drum. You begin to lose confidence in your time-tried skill as a fly fisherman, and I submit that nothing is more doleful than a male fisherman with an inferiority complex attributable to this cause. Here, I am speaking for myself alone. But consider Ollie, poor wretch! Drastically trimmed by his wife, a thing under which few if any husbands can bear up.

For example, one day at Indian Falls, Ollie brought in one of the most superb trout I have ever laid eyes on. Three pounds and eleven ounces on the scales. Ollie's star appeared to be in the ascendancy, and we rallied around to admire the fish, when Jim Black sidled up and drawled: "Well, Miz' Rodman, she didn't fish none at all today."

During the last two hours of daylight, on the last day of the trip, the male sex almost came into its glory. After supper, I walked with Lloyd to the upper pitch of Indian Falls, one of the finest pools on this fantas-

tically beautiful river. The sky was gold with the fore-
runners of a summer sunset, and the smoky haze of late
afternoon hung in the air. I cast indolently for a time,
standing on the ledge just below the falls, moved more
by the spectacle of the river than by the desire to fish.

I was using two flies on a rather heavy leader. My
dropper was a Yellow Montreal, and the point fly a
white bucktail with a gold-ribbed body. Trailing at
the edge of the pool in shallow water, the Montreal
attracted a seven-inch trout, and the little fellow
hooked himself, and made for the depths beneath the
edge of the whitewater, quite unaware that he would
have been released. It was his last mistake.

The sun slanted its bronze rays full upon him as
he darted; and, while I watched, out from under the
foam came the seven pounder! He nailed the little
trout crosswise in his mouth, and vanished under the
suds!

Lloyd Black, standing at my elbow, unloosed such
an earsplitting cry that I nearly toppled off the ledge.
Then all was still except the song of the rapids and
the drumbeat in my heart. My line ran from the top
guide-ring on a long slant straight to the center of the
pool. I stood there, keeping a steady strain for about
five minutes. Then the line came up, sluggishly.

The little trout still hung to the dropper fly, but he
was quite dead, and showed plainly the lacerations of

the big fellow's teeth. I had never witnessed such a cannibalistic performance, but I am told it is frequent on the Nepisiquit. They call the sacrifice-trout "slave fish."

I sat down on the ledge and drew a long breath. I was beginning to figure out a plan of campaign when Ollie showed up—and the light was borne upon me. He, and he alone, should catch that huge trout for the glory of mankind.

"Sit down," I said to him, solemnly.

He sat, and, after clearing my throat, I continued: "Ollie, you and I went to school together, didn't we?"

"Yes," he said, perplexed.

"For fifteen years we have hunted, fished, camped, and explored together, haven't we?"

"Yes."

"And once you pulled me out of the rapids when my canoe upset, didn't you?"

"Yes. What about it?"

"Then you went and got married, and I stood up with you at your wedding, didn't I?"

"Yes."

"All right," I concluded. "Then go down and fish that pool. Work your fly along the edge of the quick water. One of us—and it better be you!—has got to trim Doro."

"Why this pool?"

"Because under the edge of the foam," I said, pointing a shaky finger toward the whitewater, "there's a trout that will go seven pounds!"

"How do you know?"

"I had him on for five minutes."

Ollie gave an instinctive start toward the pool, hesitated, looked again, then decisively removed his hook from the keeper ring above the grip, and stepped onto the ledge. He shot his cast far out across the white feather that streaked below the falls through the center of the pool. Allowing the current to suck the fly under, he made his line loop slowly downstream and began a careful retrieve. He tried perhaps half a dozen times—then, just as his fly started upstream at the end of its loop, I saw his rod whip into a sudden curve. Ollie began to dance on the ledge. "Got him!"

He was using a five-and-three-quarter ounce Leonard Tournament, and he gave it all it would stand. Twenty minutes later, after an orgy of runs, sulks, and a pretty surface show, Ollie led the trout close to the ledge. Lying flat, I reached down and slid the net under him. But he stretched out over the rim on both sides, teetering and flopping. With one final twist, he slithered down the plane of the net, splashed back into the water, and moved off, taking his time. Dignified, austere, and, we thought, a little scornful, he swam down, down, down, until he disappeared.

There is little more to be said, this being a case where silence is particularly golden. But on the way back to camp I stopped and picked some blue gentians. They were of a delicacy and beauty worthy a champion —especially a lady champion. Rather thumb-handedly, I wove a sort of wreath and, with due ceremony, placed it that evening on Doro's head. It was very becoming, too.

"Any luck tonight in the upper pool?" she asked, looking at the garland in the cracked mirror by the lamp in Indian Falls cabin.

"None at all, dear," said her husband, thoughtfully. "We both had a strike, but we lost only one fish."

OWED TO MY SON

"BE it remembered that I, Edmund Ware Smith, of Northampton, in the Commonwealth of Massachusetts, being of sound mind and memory, but knowing the uncertainty of this life, do make this my last will and testament, hereby revoking all former wills by me at any time heretofore made.

"I bequeath and devise, as follows:

"FIRST: To my son, James Ware Smith, all my fishing tackle and equipment pertaining to fishing."

Jim: I owe you so much more than that. There are some fine Leonard rods, some Hardy reels, some English lines that cast beautifully; and to your fingers they will feel like cool velvet. And there are hosts, nay regiments, of flies; and all manner of gear and accoutrements. It is possible even that my Scotch waders will fit you, but you'll need new soles of felt on my wading shoes. But what am I trying to say to you? What indeed? I am leaving you my fishing tackle, not because it is the world's finest, but because I love you.

And there is another reason, more articulate: I have a curious conceit—but it is an honest one, I know, and I think it is wholesome, too. I want you to remember me as something a great deal more than the tall man who said "No!" too much; who said "Hurry!" when you were already struggling mightily with your shoe laces.

But those times I called you off the stream and made you go to bed were justified. You needed sleep. I could tell by the great dark hollows of your eyes, and once the no-see-ums had bitten you so that your ears swelled alarmingly, but you said: "Oh, don't make me come in! There's a big trout under the rock, Dad! I *saw* him!" I made you go into the club house to bed, and later I came in and saw you fast asleep with all your clothes on, and you were hugging the pillow pretty desperately, I thought.

So when I made out my will, I left you my fishing tackle—to remember me by. The lawyer chuckled when I told him, but I didn't. He said: "That's rather nice," but you will know that it goes far, far deeper than that. You always had unusual discernment, and I remember the first time I noticed it in you. In the club diary, which runs steadily since 1872, there's an entry by an unknown deer hunter. I read it to you one night. It goes like this:

"Buried poor old mother today, and was a gude turn-out despit cold. Flours was ver loveli. Our only constellation is her worries in this life is over. Cloudy, good trackin snow, wind NE."

You said: "It's funny, only it isn't funny." Do you remember that?

It's very strange: in wondering what you will remember about me, I find I am simply remembering *you*. When you were eight, you were allowed to come on the Spring trip with your grandfather, other adults, and me. It must have been a miserable time for you, because all the grownups fished in the best places, and you took what was left over. No one had taken a salmon for days. It was one of those times when the stream just died out on us, and you were standing on the abutment making very good practice casts, when a salmon rose and you hooked him. We all ran toward you—grandfather, Andy, Roy, Harley, and the rest of us. I have no idea where you acquired your poise—certainly not from me. But if you invented it for the occasion, it was a splendid job. Our shouted advice, frequently conflicting, did not apparently disturb you, although you were a little white.

Grandfather held the long-handled net in readiness, and when the salmon came within reach he made a wild scoop and missed. He missed three times, and this must have impressed you, for you took time to whisper in my ear, as I stood beside you: "Dad, what in hell is wrong with Gramp?" On the fourth try, your grand-father got the fish, and as he told me later, it was only by the grace of God.

I wish there were some flash of insight, some truly valid bit of wisdom I could leave with you. But there isn't—except that there is goodness in living, in liv-ing quietly and slowly enough to savor the goodness. Mother and I used to read your letters from Deer-field with a passionate and quivering interest. We dug deep between the lines, searching for your troubles, hopes, and discoveries. They were extraordinary let-ters, we thought, especially the ones about measles and fishing.

> The Bement School
> Deerfield, Mass.
> May 18

Dear Mother:

I have had the best fun on the week end I have ever had for a long time. Sunday, Clinton, Dickie and Johnny, Rickie and I we all went fishing we fished all the way from Falls River to the Vermont line and I'll bet you don't know how many fish we caught? We caught 14 trout!!! Did we have fun! The black flies and mousqutoes were so terrific that my head is so full of lumps that I can hardly scratch it. I went through brambles and bushes that it isn't even funny. We are going swimming today. Love, Jim.

Dear Mother:

I want to tell you something very important you can get German measles twice in the same year because I got them now what do you think of that. Sunday when Cap and I were in bed, oh I didn't tell that Cap had the German measles too, he has, and we had swell fun skwirting homemade lemonaid all over the place. I forgot to tell you something again. Sunday all the boys went fishing except Cap and I and they caught over fifteen trout all together the luckies.

Love, Jim.

But the one you wrote later from Maine, when we were there on a trip together, makes me remember very intensely:

July 1st
Dobsis Lake
Maine

Dear Mother:

Yesterday Dad and I went an awful hard trip to Fourth Lake and I'll bet you can't guess what we saw. We saw the huggest bob cat we ever saw in our lives. Dad thought it was a lynx but only he knew lynxes were probly exstink here. We also caught some wonderful pickerel at the mouth of Unknown Stream.

Love, Jim.

I remember that bobcat. He came up silently over the hoss-back on the Fourth Lake Carry and stood poised with his great forepaws on a blowdown, and when I yelled he vanished. We ran ahead for another glimpse of him on the open ridge, but he was gone like a gray ghost. Wasn't he wonderful? And do you remember much about those pickerel at the mouth of Unknown Stream? We floated there in the canoe, and you looked at the setting sun, and at the last purple rhodora. The sky flamed with a quietness all its own, and the spruces of Unknown Ridge were dark and irregular. The may flies danced and died. A loon laughed, and gave its long wilderness call, and you said: "I wisht I knew what that loon was saying, Dad."

"So do I."

"Lemme see the big pickerel—the one I caught."

I got the fish out from under the stern of the canoe and held it up.

"Slide him up to me. I want to touch him."

I did, and you picked him up and glanced at the other three. "This one's biggest," you said.

"Sure, Skipper."

"I caught him, didn't I?"

"Sure you did."

That seemed to establish a kind of tranquillity in you, and you sighed. Your face was sunburned, bronze-red, and I couldn't think of any place in the world I'd rather be than right there where we were, on that day we saw the bobcat in the early twilight.

Jim, do you remember dashing madly into the house

one cold and foggy Spring and shouting: "Dad! Geese! Come quick! You can just only hear them, but not see them in the fog!" And how about the first white perch you caught? You pounced upon him all too eagerly, snatched your hand away, and thrust your finger into your mouth. You looked at me as if I had played a scurvy trick on you, then removed your finger and said: "You should of told me they had prickers, father!"

You were so wonderful when you were first learning to cast a plug lure. You had got the hang of it, and you'd shoot out a tremendous side-arm cast, and while the plug was sailing out you'd be watching me to assure yourself that I was looking. I *was* looking!

I have remembered these things a thousand times; remembered them flying in moonlight above clouds; remembered them in strange little towns full of dust and boasting; remembered them leaning on a fence in Spring, smelling the damp meadow and listening to remote tendrils of music from young frogs.

But—what will *you* remember? Will you think again of the perch in the pond where willows grew? Will you remember how the turtles floated with just their noses sticking out? Remember how the smoke from the fire went straight up, lost in the sky above our island? And the redwing blackbirds, merry in the cat-tails? And will you try to love the sound of a freight train in the night, and call it the long-journey-sound? Jim! These things are all yours. Look closely at them. They are good!

Where and what is the essence I am seeking? Sometimes, somberly, I remember that you gave me more than I gave you—and it should have been the other way around. Here, I am not even giving you decent brook-bank philosophy. And my last will and testament bequeaths you little more than some second-hand fishing tackle in excellent repair. Where is the word I am after? It must mean part gratitude to you, and for you; and part prayer that you will inherit meanings I know are here, but cannot even remotely express. I am thinking of sun and wind and honesty. I am thinking of moving water, the Fifth Machias burn, and the feel of smooth stones underfoot. I am thinking of the fluid stillness of a canoe on Second Chain deadwater. I am thinking of the destination of your life, and of the hard work, the good work, required to achieve it rightly. I am thinking of a few brief moments when a man is overwhelmed and inspired by an awareness of the universe around him. Good luck, boy. I realize I have left you nothing you do not already possess.

THE HERO WORSHIP OF
SAM BUSBY

I KNEW, of course, that Alonzo Parsons was a human being. So did all other members of the Cape Cod Trout Club—all, that is, except Samuel Q. Busby. Sam felt that Alonzo was a god. His worship of the angling skill of Alonzo was once a byword at the club. I don't say that Sam would actually bow when Alonzo came into the dining room of the Old Colony Inn, the club headquarters at Wareham, Massachusetts—but clearly Sam regarded the gruff and accomplished old fly fisherman as he might have regarded the shade of the late great Halford.

I am quite certain that Sam Busby is a type. He was born into the predicament of doubting himself and believing all others. He would set any greater angler on a pedestal, believing him to be without flaw in all things. But invariably the pedestal topples, the idol falls and the human being prevails, and is not so very flawless after all. Sadly, then, the Sam Busbys perceive the cruelty of life and of fishing, realizing that they worshiped something which was not there, and could not be. This is the story, in Sam's own yearning words, of his awakening.

I was soaking a leader below the spring near Phillips' camp on Eagle Hill Stream, when I heard sounds of awkwardness behind me and glanced 'round to discover Sam waddling down the bluff in his waders. "Hello—hoping I'd find you here," he said. "Good day for a Greenwell's Glory, don't you think?"

"I never can tell which fly to start with, Sam," I answered. "What makes you partial to the Reverend Canon Greenwell's creation?"

Sam's face clouded. His mustache vibrated, and his eyes bulged outward until I thought they might touch the lenses of his horn-rimmed glasses. "It's because of an experience I had," he said. Glancing about, he made certain that we were alone. "If you've got a minute," he went on, "I'll tell you about it. I guess I can tell it— now. Alonzo Parsons has moved to California, permanently." Sam's voice was absurdly high, and intense, and as his theme rounded in his bosom, it was as if he were disturbed by some dire question involving international diplomacy, or love.

"My leader ought to be soaked now," I hinted.

But Sam didn't hear. He settled himself on the stern seat of a beached rowboat, and began:

As Montaigne said nearly four hundred years ago (Sam was off to an academic start!), "One seldom speaks of one's self without detriment to the person spoken of." Yet in the very echo of the old Frenchman's apothegm, I am going to be perfectly straightforward in matters concerning the big rainbow, the Greenwell's Glory flies, and my fishing trip with Alonzo Parsons. I simply offer the virtue of an honest confession against whatever detriment may accrue. You shall judge.

(Here Sam pressed his palm to his forehead, closed his eyes, opened them, and took up his tale in earnest.)

The man in the street imagines that among anglers a sort of blanket social equality prevails. I disagree. Certainly at the Cape Cod Trout Club, during the brief reign of Alonzo Parsons, nothing was further from the truth. Then the caste system held sway. The high caste numbered those who had fished with Alonzo. The low caste, those who had not. Before Alonzo left, I fished—that is, *almost* fished with him.

"I didn't hear him mention it, Sam," I interposed.

"You never will," said Busby, hollowly.

"Why? Why shouldn't he mention it?"

"He didn't know it."

"How could you fish—or, as you say, almost fish—with a man without his knowing it? Especially an old hawk like Alonzo Parsons?"

"If you will just bear with me, I will explain everything," said Sam, brushing a beetle from his sleeve.

I have told you, of course, of the—uh—zeal with which I have—well, pursued the elusive Parsons. For five seasons I have longed to fish in his company, on Eagle Hill Stream—here. Oh, I know my casting technique is sloppy. But a day with Alonzo would have given me the confidence I always lack. Just to work the stream with him for one evening's fishing! He seemed to know more about where trout lie, and what they feed on, and when, than any living man. There was a time when the whole membership of the club followed, as it were, in the wake of his advice. "Is Parsons on the stream? If so, we'll go, too." Or, "Alonzo fished dry today. Guess I will, too." Or, "He's gone to Rose Brook Pond. They must be rising there." The man was supernatural in his judgment.

Once I got him alone in the club dining room, and said: "Alonzo, let's try the upper part of the stream this evening. Just the two of us—together?"

He uncoiled from his chair, stood up, grabbed his hat, said: "No. Wind's East," and departed.

Another time, on a perfect June afternoon, I tried him again: "Les' Handy says there's a hatch of fly, Alonzo. Will you try the evening fishing—with me?"

"Expecting a friend," he replied, looking up rather

brusquely from a card which contained Sturdy's table of weights.

Well, three winters ago, you'll remember I got the fly tying bug. At first I turned out some frightful specimens, but early last spring I suddenly found the knack, got hold of something really fine in the way of hackle feathers, and tied a dozen Greenwell's Glory fanwings on short-shanked No. 14 hooks. They were the best—and the last—I ever tied. At the very first opportunity, I presented them to Alonzo, saying casually: "Take these and try them some time. I think you may like the way they float."

"Give 'em to someone that likes fanwings. I don't," he said.

About a month later, toward the first of May, last, I got two dozen Quill Gordons and Light Cahills from that genius down in Morgantown, West Virginia—Joe Messinger, his name is. They say Joe has hands like a blacksmith, uses a spring clothespin for a vise, and in thirty seconds ties a fly that will float over Niagara Falls. The day the flies came I ate lunch alone in the Somerset Club in Boston. While I waited for my order, I opened the box of flies and arranged them on the table cloth in front of me. I was sort of dreaming over them, when a voice said: "God! Did you tie *those?*"

I looked around. Directly back of my right shoulder, his eyes a gleaming steel-gray, stood Alonzo Parsons. I don't know what made me say it, but I said it, and once said, there was no retracting it. I said: "Yes—I tied them."

Alonzo took a step forward, bent over the table, reached out a slow hand, then withdrew it as from temptation.

"Go ahead and take your pick," I told him.

He looked at me, blinking: "You mean it?"

"Yes."

He removed a box from his side coat pocket, and selected six each of the Gordons and the Cahills. "Meet me on Eagle Hill Stream at six this evening," he said, and walked briskly away.

I was so excited I had a double brandy to steady myself. Then I began to think clearly, and to sort out certain obstacles that stood in my way. The first, and paramount, was, if I may say so, Mrs. Busby. She had some sort of tickets to some sort of play some sort of local theatrical group was giving. And my fishing tackle, of course, was at home. To drive out home and get my tackle would be sheer folly—putting one's head on the guillotine, so to speak. But to call her up, tell her I had been called away, and my fishing tackle at home in the closet—ah! You see? Practically the perfect alibi. Mrs. Busby is the sort of woman who—did I ever tell you about the time I cleaned the salmon in the bathroom?

"Yes—yes, Sam. I know about that," I said hastily.

Or (he went on) about the time I was testing leaders? I drove a nail into the window casing, and looped the leaders over it to get a good, steady, straight pull. It was just a small nail, but—

"But in driving it into the casing, you missed it several times, and dented the casing? You told me about that, Sam."

Oh, did I? Forgot! (he said, bewilderedly). Where was I? Yes. Got it now. Somerset Club. Well, anyway, I called up Mrs. Busby. It worked perfectly. I told her I had to go to Portland on the Pine Tree Limited, and wouldn't be home until the next day. She said "Yes? Wait just a minute, Samuel." Then I heard her step away from the phone. I have no doubt she went to make sure that my tackle was at home. When she took up the phone again, she said it was all right, that I could go. So I went up to Dame-Stoddard's and bought a whole new outfit—but only a few flies. I had some of the Greenwell's Glories I had tied in my desk at the office, and the remaining Messinger Cahills and Gordons in my pocket. The new outfit set me back seventy-five dollars, counting leaders, reel, line, and a rather nicely balanced little Thomas rod. Then there were waders, wading shoes, net and basket. In all, I must have spent a hundred and fifteen dollars. But it didn't seem like anything.

I was feverish all afternoon. At four I called Parsons and asked him if he'd like to drive down in my car. He said: "No. Go in my own."

"Well—look, Alonzo. Where'll we meet?"

"On the stream. I said on the stream," he replied, and hung up.

I set up the Thomas, fitted the reel and did ceiling practice until four-thirty. I was afraid that my new line was too light for the combination, but it was too late to change now. It was just that I wanted to be in good wrist while fishing with Parsons. I soaked some nine-foot leaders, got my few flies arranged in two round pyralin boxes, and started for Wareham.

There are three good entrances to Eagle Hill Stream. The first is here at Phillips' camp. Farther up, about a mile, is what we call the Second Landing. Still farther up is another landing where you can park close to the stream.

I decided my best bet was the Second Landing. Obviously Alonzo Parsons would fish dry—with Joe Messinger's flies. I would start at the Second Landing, and work down, certain of meeting him along the way. I was in the stream at the Second Landing at 5:45—a beautiful, nearly windless afternoon.

The shadowed, historic little river ran in the twilight of its own trees. A rich, golden, bee-humming twilight. I felt the water cool against my new waders, as I stepped carefully to the far side. Right there, at the Second Landing, is one of the finest pools. The current, sliding along soundlessly, hits the right bank, rolls back to the left. The water is perhaps four feet deep, and clear. It is a difficult pool to fish, for any but the most skilful casters. Back of your right shoulder is a maple tree—in direct line with a proper backcast. It is almost impossible to make an effective roll cast, because of the way the stream bends. You must cast a short line to fish the pool correctly, and to roll cast a short line with a very light nine-foot leader is next to impossible—even if you don't take into consideration the commotion you are likely to make on the surface.

I stood there, taking it all in, looking now and then downstream, and listening for Alonzo Parsons. It was not quite six, and I figured I would meet him by the Log Pool, below, at about half past.

Did you ever feel, welling up in you, a curious gratitude to your surroundings, and to the fact that you are among them? Oh, I know it sounds foolish—but Daniel Webster had fished this stream, and the late Calvin Coolidge, and Jack Sharkey—and Alonzo Parsons! I seemed to partake of the assorted greatness of these men. I tingled pleasantly with an atmosphere of—well, immortality. An oriole drifted through the branches of a solitary elm. A light breeze fanned my cheek, and swayed my leader. Then I heard the splash!

Technically, it was not a splash. Only small trout make a splash, as they punch up through the surface. This sound was like that one's guide will sometimes make with a sudden, strong, stroke of his paddle. It is made by an abrupt bulging up of the water. I stared at the ripple which carried almost across the stream from the pool not thirty feet away. Under some bushes, a few small may flies were hatching—rather light in color. I watched one touch the surface, rise, touch again—and then I saw the trout. That is, I saw a part of his tail, and the rich red-pink stripe of the rainbow, just under the surface.

To take a rainbow of this size on a dry fly, while fishing with—or practically with—Alonzo Parsons, was almost like a dream of perfection. I stood there, shaking, my mind making curious little stabs of projection into a future—wherein the Club members clustered around our table at dinner, mutely admiring the trout. And I was there to tell them the tale, coolly, and with dignity, while Alonzo Parsons, beside me, nodded the wordless corroboration of the angling great.

Unless you are a fisherman, you cannot possibly realize a man's sensation when he has a trout like this practically in his basket. It does something to you. Your mouth goes cottony, and your knees seem to buckle. And every move you make is deathly slow. Whether it was this, or the strange rod, I cannot say. My first backcast fouled in the branches of that accursed maple tree, behind my right shoulder.

I broke the leader. To wade ashore and climb the tree would certainly disturb the water. Besides, I was in a hurry. I took a hasty glance downstream. I listened. There was no evidence of Alonzo Parsons. With unsteady fingers, I removed a fly box and tied on another Light Cahill. Before I got the cover back on the box, a vagrant puff of wind sort of bumped several of the flies out of the box. I grabbed, and missed, and box and all went into the stream. By great good fortune, they sailed downstream on the near side—well out of range of the feeding rainbow. I let them go. I still had what were left of the original dozen Greenwell's Glories I had tied.

This time I tried a low backcast, preparing to make a delicate slack-cast. The current was slow, perfect for a slack-cast. But I hung in a confounded alder, just as the great trout boiled beneath the surface again and took one of the naturals.

I broke my leader again, and from now on it was my Greenwell's Glories. Three times I had seen, or heard the trout rise, and I had not yet got a fly over him! It was almost impossible for me to tie knots in my nervous condition. Gone were my sensations of peace and plenitude. I was in the exact center of a chance of a lifetime, and I was muffing it. And—oh, *hell!*

[69]

My watch said 6:26, and I thought I heard the faint splash of Alonzo wading through a shallow stretch two hundred yards below. I looked, but could see nothing. And I put four Greenwell's Glories into that unholy maple frond, twenty feet above my head. Another went on a cedar snag. The wind carried it. Aside from that, the cast was perfect. I mean, it simply didn't reach the water.

I am not wholly lucid on events immediately following this. I think there was a kind of panic, the kind which nature happily blots from one's memory, as being too difficult for the human brain to withstand. But some moments later, I started to tie on another Greenwell's, and found the box empty!

It must have been the rainbow's fourth or fifth boiling rise that brought me to my senses. My reflection in the slow, smooth water reminded me of something hewn from cheese. I looked back at the maple tree. Now and then a breeze would stir the topmost branch —the one over the stream—and I would see a glint of light on the fag ends of several leaders. There was nothing to do but climb the tree and pluck myself some Greenwell's Glories.

The actual climbing required all my strength, what with waders and basket. I found the precious limb, and was crawling toward it, reaching, when I heard the unmistakable sound of a man wading the shallows.

Peering out between the leafy branches, I saw Alonzo Parsons! I muttered a faint prayer that he had seen no untoward commotion in the maple limbs, and lay stock still, hanging on for dear life. No! He had not seen me. Some strange spark of sportsmanship prompted me to cry out to him that he was nearing the largest trout that ever rose to take a drake. But I bit the words back. You can hardly blame me. What would Alonzo think, or say, when he saw me up the tree? You cannot tell so exalted a caster as Alonzo that you are up a tree to pluck yourself some flies. You cannot tell him—and expect him to believe—that you are up there to enjoy the sunset, or the view. No. The thing to do is to remain the patient, precarious, tree-dweller until Alonzo has passed.

Alonzo, now almost directly below me—not twenty yards away—stopped short. The great rainbow had rolled up in his feeding. A grim and predatory smile broke upon Alonzo Parsons' lips. My heart sank, and I wanted to close my eyes, as Alonzo positioned himself and began to lengthen line over the pool. His fly dropped like down from under the wing of a small bird. It drifted down toward him—he was below the pool, and casting upstream. It passed over the trout. The trout ignored it. I—well, I might as well admit it—I was glad. Why should he catch my trout?

He tried again, and the trout remained faithful to

me. Parsons' face clouded. His smile vanished. He looked upstream, then downstream, then cast again—almost viciously. I practically adored the trout for refusing Alonzo's art. He kept on for fifteen or twenty minutes, his face getting grimmer and grimmer. I saw him look furtively about him and listen. Then he muttered something under his breath, and waded—I say, he waded ashore and sat down.

From an inner pocket of his fishing vest—and I could actually see the glint in the last rays of the sun—he, Alonzo Parsons, removed an aluminum box. And from the box, he extracted a *spinner!* Yes, a spinner!

(I was actually excited myself. One couldn't help it. Busby's face was beaded with moisture. "Then what did he do?" I asked. Busby licked his lips. I could have sworn I heard his tongue rustling in his dry mouth.)

What did he do? (he said, limply.) What did he do? He pulled up a damp sod, broke it apart, and dragged from it a worm! And he fixed the worm to the hook beneath the spinner, and tied the works to a heavy leader, and the leader to his tapered line. And he caught my rainbow trout.

"And then, what?" I asked.

He took down his rod, concealed his spinner, creeled my trout in a nest of wet ferns, and sneaked away on the woods road, toward Phillips' camp, where, apparently, he had left his car.

"But—Sam," I said. "The Club calls for fly fishing only. You could have him black-balled for a stunt like that."

Wait! I got back to the Old Colony Inn after dark, and there at the center table sat Alonzo Parsons, and in front of him was a huge platter on which lay the rainbow—my rainbow. The cluster of anglers, which I had imagined at one time would surround me, were in reality surrounding Alonzo. He was describing, probably for the eighth time, just how he took the fish. According to Parsons, it was like this:

"I was coming up to the Second Landing Pool, when I saw the big fellow bulge the surface after a may fly. I was using a Quill Gordon, but changed to a Light Cahill, and took him on about the fourth cast. I was over twenty minutes getting the net under him."

Here Parsons pointed to the trout's mouth. "There," he said. "There's the fly—you can see it. It's a No. 14, tied by—" Then he looked up and saw me.

"There's Busby, now! He's the fellow that tied that Cahill! Prettiest I ever put down on any water. And—*say*, Busby!" Alonzo frowned at me, his steel-gray eyes transfixing me. He said: "I thought I had a date to meet you on the stream. Where the hell have you been?"

I stood swallowing. It was lie for lie—mine about tying the flies that Joe Messinger tied; and Alonzo

Parsons' about catching a trout that a worm caught. I knew his secret. But to expose it was to put myself—figuratively and literally—up a tree. I could anticipate the entire dialogue. It would be like this. I would point at Parsons, and say: "I *saw* you catch that rainbow!"

Parsons: "Oh, you did? Well, where were you?"

Me: "I was up a tree."

Amid general laughter, Parsons would say: "What were you doing up there?"

Me: "Picking some Greenwell's Glories."

Parsons, his great voice roaring above the laughter: "Oh—so they grow on trees, do they? Haw-haw-haw!"

So actually I simply stared at him, smiling a little, and I said: "Alonzo, I'm sorry, but I was detained." Then I went out into the night and drove home. I—

"Was Mrs. Busby surprised to see you ahead of schedule, Sam?"

Sam straightened up on the stern seat of the rowboat. "Well—no. She said she wasn't, that is. She said she'd expected it all along. But she—she said that if I was going to sneak off fishing again, when I had a date with her, that I ought to have enough sense not to come home with my waders on."

THE UNINVITED PEST

In the pine-shadowed twilight of the lake shore near Paul Kegan's camps in Ontario, I was quietly recovering from a grouch. Fishing had been unusually poor, lunch had been eaten in the neighborhood of an ant hill, and I had lost a Hardy reel. But over these woes the curtain of peace was descending. A loon called from midlake, a trout broke off shore, and my childish sulk had slowly evaporated—when Samuel Q. Busby arrived, and sat down beside me in an invulnerable mood of narrative.

There is nothing pagan or immoral about Busby, but he has developed to a high degree the knack of appearing at the wrong time. He is one of those fellows you forget instantly until the next time he shows up, and then he makes you want to go away somewhere. But you can't, and you wouldn't, for fear of wounding him. He wears his troubles on the sleeve of his coat, and is usually groping for sympathy in a way no man can resist.

"Hello!" he cried, enthusiastically. "Just the man I wanted to talk to."

"Have you noticed the stillness?" I inquired. "It's delightful, Sam—good for the soul."

"I've got to tell someone about what my wife did to me," he bubbled. "I believe you are one of the few men who can understand."

"I suppose the Almighty invented silence to fill us mortals with a sense of peace."

"It's about a fishing trip," pursued Busby, "and it was indirectly her fault."

"Have you felt that at twilight, the silence seems to have an especial depth and beauty?" But it was a futile question. Busby hadn't, at the moment.

He was a rotund little man, much smaller physically than his wife. She was of the militant or warhorse type whose most trifling utterances come upon the ear with the dreamy, wistful emphasis of a drophammer. Perhaps it was because of this that poor Sam seemed to be in a continual state of retreat. He loved fishing with an almost fantastic passion; and when, as now, he was preparing to talk about it, he suggested a frustrated bee seeking nectar among the skunk cabbages. Or, if you noted only his protruding eyes and scattering mustache he more closely resembled an habitually astonished walrus. No more tender-hearted person ever lived—but, as I sighed and settled back against a pine trunk, the will to listen to him was not in me.

The logic of womankind (he began, in a portentous voice) is best represented by the cipher, the cipher being symbolic of the goose egg, or nothing at all. (Here Busby shaped his fingers in a way which I took to signify the center portion of a doughnut. His conclusions on the subject of women were unhappily based upon experience with a single specimen, which he had the misfortune to marry.)

Consider the following breakfast table conversation (he continued, in a stunned tone), always bearing in mind that breakfast, traditionally, should be a silent meal, disturbed only by the crunching of toast.

On the morning of which I speak, Mrs. Busby skewered me with a stare from across the table, and said: "Samuel—" She is not the woman to shorten it to Sam. "Samuel," she said, "where do you propose to spend your vacation this year, dear?"

Between ourselves (Busby glanced at the darkening pines, and lowered his voice furtively) Mrs. Busby gets a nuance into the word "dear" which makes it no more a term of affection than thief, idiot, or worm. But let it pass.

At the moment of her question, I was engaged in chewing shredded wheat, so it is barely possible that she misunderstood my answer, which was: "Fishing. Trout. Maine."

"Won't it be nice," she replied, with a certain re-enforced decisiveness. "You and little Wilfred—going off fishing, *together!*"

You understand now, don't you, why I thought she might not have heard me correctly? And why I began my narrative with an observation on female logic? I had not mentioned the "pest," as I secretly designated little Wilfred. And of course I did not see eye-to-eye with Mrs. Busby in the matter of taking him fishing with me, and I will tell you why:

The pest, aged seven, is the only son of one of my wife's college friends. The college friend had gone to Europe, and, since we are a childless couple, Mrs. Busby had offered to house, feed, and otherwise endure the pest for six weeks. Of course I had not been consulted. I am the sort of husband who—er—uh—is never consulted about anything by the—uh—sort of woman a man like me usually marries. Am I clear?

At the very moment of which I speak, the pest sat across the table from me. He was making rather a rough job of eating an egg. In a spirit possibly of sheer alchemy, he had mixed the egg with a dish of pre-served quinces. An alert eye could detect traces of both fruits in the pest's hair, and all along down his bib-front to his waist.

Returning Mrs. Busby's stare, I said quietly: "I do not intend to take him fishing with me, dear. He is not old enough. He might—"

Mrs. Busby pounced upon me—verbally, that is. When she is disturbed, or crossed, that is the way her words come. They pounce. She said: "Samuel, don't speak that way in front of little Wilfred. You'll wound his sensitive feelings."

"Impossible," I sighed, thoughtlessly. "He has none."

"*Samuel!*" she said to me. "He is a very sensitive child."

"I understand, dear, that rattlesnakes are also sensitive," was my rejoinder.

Here Mrs. Busby leaned forward and regarded me with what I am obliged to call a beady glare. "Are you calling Wilfred—Irma's little boy—a *rattlesnake?*"

"My dear, of course not," I disclaimed. "What on earth made you think that?"

"My ears," she said, with the tigerish vigor of which she alone is capable.

"Anyway," I announced, steadfastly, "the pest will not go on my fishing trip. It's my vacation."

"Hah!" she said, getting in the ultimate thrust.

On the following Monday morning, we—that is, the pest and I—were met at Bear Trap Landing, Maine, by the two guides I had engaged for the fishing trip. On the train going up, the pest had insisted on sleeping in the lower berth with me. He seemed tirelessly to enjoy a practice he defined as "horseback riding." I am not a horse, but this was a trifling drawback. He straddled me and rode amiably until the breath had departed from my lungs. Then he leaned over and raised the curtain to look out at the stars.

He awoke me at Salem, Portsmouth, Portland and Bangor by prodding me in the stomach, and saying: "What are we stopping for?" I had attempted to give him a blanket answer by saying that every time the train stopped it did so to take on passengers. But when it stopped at Mattawamkeag, the pest awoke me to impart this information: "No one got on. One man got off. Hah!"

I think it was about at this time that I was reminded of Sir James Barrie's pungent apothegm on work. "Nothing is really work," he said, "unless you would rather be doing something else." In the light of Sir James' remark, I marvelled at my own industry. It shamed that of the ant and the bee.

But here we were on the river bank, shaking hands with George and Pud. It enriched me to see again these faithful friends, to inquire as to the health of themselves and their families, and to hear of the likelihood of good fishing. The pest had wandered down to the water's edge, but peace reigned only for a moment. It was shattered by what sentimental novelists refer to as a "glad outcry." When we reached him, the pest pointed down into the water. We were in time to see the shadowy form of a huge eel. By some diabolic intuition, the pest had evidently divined my psychopathic aversion to eels. "Uncle Buzz," he shouted, enraptured, "would you eat an eel if I caught one?"

The suggestion gave me a distinctly unpleasant moment. "No, Wilfred. I would not."

The pest immediately puckered, and burst into tears.

"Shush, Wilfred," I consoled. "There, there now."

He increased his flow of tears at once, and introduced a brand of caterwauling hitherto unknown to human ears. It was his mettle against mine—and mine weakened, as I caught the pleading looks in the eyes of George and Pud. I estimated the pest's probabilities of catching an eel at about one in a thousand, and was willing to take the chance. "All right," I said. "I agree." He quieted into a kind of sniffling sulk.

After arranging the duffel in the two canoes, we started upstream, the pest in dear old George's canoe and separated from me by twenty blessed yards of open water. The last I saw of him until noon, he was in the bow of George's craft, standing up, and paddling violently backwards. I saw George plead with him, then bow his head in despair. In a shrill, remonstrating voice, the pest was pointing out with some logic that by

[81]

paddling backwards he was able to create a bigger wave upon the water.

Pud and I hung back until they disappeared, then sided in toward the Lower Mopang pool with mutual sighs of relief. I took plenty of time setting up my rod and soaking a nine-foot leader. The leader point calibrated only five thousandths, and I remember wondering at the time if this weren't a trifle fine. My nervous, over-eager strikes of early season are frequently disastrous to fine gut. But of course I never dreamed that a crisis was at hand. One never does, unhappily.

I had tied on a Wickham's No. 12, oiled it, and was making an experimental cast of less than twenty feet to determine how the fly would float. About to pick up the fly, I saw a bronze shape boil up under it, and struck instinctively. The leader parted just an inch or so above the fly, and a second later the fly itself appeared on the surface drifting down toward us! "Pud," I said, in an awed voice. "Did you see that?"

"Gawd A'mighty, yes!"

I don't know why it is that a fisherman, after he has pricked and lost a heavy trout, will persist in casting over the same water again. Experience and good sense tell him that the trout will not return, at least on the same day. This is especially true of brown and rainbow trout. Although this fish was a squaretail, I don't suppose I had any real hope of tempting him again. But I tried him with a Pink Lady, and after ten minutes careful casting, he came again, and I hooked him.

Pud is not an excitable guide, but when he got his first full look at this magnificent fish, he strung together with beautiful unity and coherence practically all of the words which, in the Old Testament itself, are studiously scattered. His skilful handling of the canoe was all that saved the trout for me—and this trout was one of the few that I truly *wanted*. He weighed three pounds, nine ounces, and I have taken larger trout, say in some of the wilderness rivers of the Albany watershed in the Hudson's Bay region. But I never saw a more beautiful trout from the standpoint of shape, color, and condition. For a good many years I had wanted such a trout as this to mount and hang in my study. I do not like a lot of trophies. I like a few very good ones. In this trout, I had the perfect specimen. Rather than prepare him here, we decided to bring him to camp where Pud had a scalpel, and where we could pack him properly. Tenderly we arranged a sepulchre of wet moss and ferns. Tenderly we wrapped the trout in a clean white undershirt, slightly moistened. I sighed deeply. Never had the spruces and pines, the swirling waters, and the mile-high clouds looked so good to me.

During the entire episode I had, of course, forgotten the pest; but of a sudden I was reminded of him by a whistling sound. I didn't at first attribute the whistling to the pest. It simply reminded me of him because it was poisonously grating and unpleasant, and not at all in keeping with the serenity of the river. The note was peculiarly sharp, and produced the kind of prickling shudder one might expect when stepping barefoot into a cache of old razor blades.

Then, rounding a bend, I perceived that the sound came in a sense from little Wilfred himself. George, my weathered companion of many a campfire, loyal through storm and strife, lay flat upon his back, hands covering his ears, eyes tight shut in misery, while blast upon blast issued from a large willow whistle which, in a deranged moment, he had fashioned for the pest with a jackknife.

The instant he spotted our canoe, the pest uttered a series of screeches, his words interspersed at maddening intervals with blasts on the whistle: "You're—*sr-sr-sr*—late—*sr-sr-sr*—Uncle Buzz. *Sr-sr-sr*—"

I cannot hope to describe to you the sense of disharmony he managed to get into his "*Sr-sr-sr*." It should not be ascribed alone to George's ill luck in shaping the whistle. I am more of the belief that little Wilfred imparted some fiendish effect of his own. I gulped, and said to him: "Wilfred, we've got the most beautiful trout I have ever seen."

"Let's—*sr-sr-sr*—see him."

[84]

Reverently I unswathed the trout, almost hating to expose its defenseless though unhearing ears to the agony of the whistle.

"*Sr-sr-sr*—" shrilled the pest. "I've seen—*sr-sr-sr* —codfish bigger'n that—*sr-sr*."

"Wilfred," I beseeched him, ignoring his insult, "please stop whistling."

"*Sr-sr-sr*—nope—*sr-sr-sr*."

"I'll give you a dollar if you'll stop."

"*Sr-sr-sr*—nope. But I'll—*sr-sr-sr*—stop for a penny. *Sr-sr*."

As one man, George, Pud and I reached into our pockets; but the tragedy only deepened when we found not a penny among us. "Here's a dime," said George. "Worth ten of what a penny is."

"*Sr-sr-sr*—penny—*sr-sr-sr*—I said—*sr-sr-sr*— penny."

He refused in turn a jackknife, a nickel, a quarter, a half dollar, and George's priceless silver badge bearing his registration as a grade-A guide, State of Maine. A sudden, if somewhat distracted inspiration seized me, and I laid a hand on the pest's scrawny shoulder. "Wilfred!" I hissed. "Will you take a check?"

"Hell—*sr-sr-sr*—no—*sr-sr*."

"You mustn't use that word," I admonished.

"*Sr-sr*—George does. Pud does. You do—*sr*."

Hope withered in my breast.

[85]

(At this point in his somber narrative, Busby leaned closer to me in the waning light, and I could almost feel the sadness oozing from his pores, as he continued.)

There is not much more to tell (he said); that is, I can scarcely bear to talk about it—yet. That noon we cooked lunch in a beautiful poplar grove—an old river-drivers' campground, it was. We built our fire some distance back from the river, and George—his wits sharpened by desperation—suggested that Wilfred go down to the river where we'd beached the canoes and wet his whistle. George told him that the note of the whistle was dying out—and the pest was off like a shot.

When the lunch was cooked, I sauntered down to the river bank and found—I want you to try to believe me, because it is the solemn truth—I found Wilfred with *my prize trout!* Even as the gooseflesh sprouted upon me, he wiped a jackknife on his pants, laid it aside, and picked up his whistle: "*Sr-sr-sr*—" he began. "I cleaned your—*sr-sr-sr*—trout, Uncle Buzz."

This was, at best, an understatement. He had lacerated that magnificent fish beyond all hope of surgery. The meat, pink and delicate, lay about on the grass in hunks of about a quarter pound in weight. I felt as if I had swallowed a quince. A kind of ague seized me: "Wilfred—for God's sake, why did you do this?"

"*Sr-sr-sr*—wanted to see what was inside of him— *sr-sr-sr*—and besides, George said that—*sr-sr-sr*— trout's insides made good bait for eels. *Sr-sr-sr*—they did, too. I caught one! *Sr-sr-sr*—"

(Poor Busby! The weight of doom was in his words, and I felt moved to lay a sympathetic hand on his shoulder. Now, for the first time, it struck me as peculiar that he had come here to Paul Kegan's camps when he was supposed to be off fishing with the pest. I asked him why.)

"Why?" echoed Busby, weakly. "I was taken ill. Had to cut the trip short. After I recovered, there were a few days left of my vacation. I managed to persuade Mrs. Busby to let me come up here—alone."

"Ill?" I inquired, solicitously. "How do you mean?"

I could hear—I *swear* I could hear—a sort of gurgling protest from the region of Busby's Adam's apple, as he moaned: "I ate the eel."

"All of it?"

"Yes—all of it."

"How much did it weigh?"

"Slightly less than three pounds, dressed."

Despite the approaching dusk, one could easily discern a strange, greenish cast on Busby's distraught countenance. "But the pest gave up the whistle," he finished, a cracked, belated, note of triumph in his voice.

LO, THE LONG BROWN RIDGES

More than a vestige of fitness inheres in "Lo, the long brown ridges." To me the words isolate an atmosphere—perhaps because, under my breath, I repeat them when I see those ridges in November. No one hears me. I would hate to be thought a fool for my awe. Even now, I can feel the lucid silence of a cedar swamp—tomblike, tangled, ancient as the Book. And above the swamp the brown ridge rests in perpetual peace. This is the ridge eastward of the peeled spruce cabin, whose walls blend more and more with the surroundings as the seasons mellow them.

Forty-one steps from the cabin door the waters of Third Chain Lake have washed the stones and lapped at the cedar roots for centuries. Evening and morning in November the white mist coils to catch the sun. You breathe its almost tangible humidity. You hear the hum of silence—so imperious that you shame at the drip of your own paddle, or the damp splutter of your pipe.

Across the lake is the greatest of the long brown ridges—Duck Lake Mountain; and another to the north; and only to southwestward is the skyline low, where the carry leads to Unknown.

We built the cabin with our own hands in a virgin stand of pine; and in a northwest wind the great trees rub against one another, moaning in their topmost branches, and keeping us fitful in our bunks, thinking of a headwind paddle next day. We built that cabin— H., and Roy, and an unknown Indian, and I. Particularly, therefore, are we endeared to the creaky floor, the tar-smell of the calking, the graying logs of its walls. Because always men have pondered preciously the graces of their own handiwork.

If anyone may be said singly to possess the cabin, it is H. That is to say, he paid for it. Yet he would hardly claim it as his own. On the contrary, it possesses him. H. is older than the rest of us. He is sixty, and the wake he has left behind him in his life is as impressive as the white track behind a liner. H. is a grandfather, and a great deal of wisdom has gathered in his head. His interest in all things on earth is insatiable, and he can love a cloud, a cardinal flower, or a human being —and sometimes he can almost explain them. He loves to hew with an axe, and loudly he berates himself when he cuts his knee. He paddles his own canoe, totes a lion's share on the carries, and he hunts the long

[90]

brown ridges alone. He asserts that his miles-per-hour, or his heavy pavement-tread in the timber would gutter the chances of a companion in getting a shot at a deer. But actually he likes to come single-handed against the wilderness. Alone, he treads on no one's heels, nor waits for the man behind him.

But in hunting alone, H. denies the rest of us the pleasure of his conversation. We look forward to evenings in the cabin, wondering what thoughts he may have had during the day's hunt.

"I believe," said H., one last night in camp while the rain dripped sleepily on the roof, "—I believe in a Unity of Things."

"Why?" I asked. If you have had no formal training in philosophy, the word "why" gives you a chance to array your thoughts. Without further prompting, H. enlarged upon his theme.

"Everything dovetails too perfectly for chance," he said, "running smoothly and perpetually in the river of cause and effect. For example, I cannot be satisfied that the great ice sheet which formed these lakes and ridges a million years ago, came at the whim of chance. Either the mind of man was fashioned purposely to regard the lakes and ridges as perfect, or the lakes and ridges came last, perfectly formed to man's eyes. In either case, you have a sort of Unity."

Roy hung a pair of damp socks on a rafter and got

out his corncob. "I never looked at it like that," he said. "But I see how you mean, H. You mean a thing don't happen just to suit you, because you might of happened just to suit *it*, an' there's no telling which."

I drew an oily rag through the barrel of my Winchester and tried to think of some argument for the opposition. To me, it was merely the ancient problem of which came first, the hen or the egg. But H.'s mind was opening up as free and hopeful as wind on a hill. His idea of Unity was pleasant to contemplate, but like all universal speculators, he was merely taking a shot in the dark at Truth.

"I don't believe the Unity idea," I said. "It's too neat. The precepts of chance suit me as well. And chance preëmpts purpose. The whole works just happened, and so did we. Where's the need of any ultimate purpose anyway, so long as each individual clings to his puny private one?"

H. grinned, and I guessed he had been laying a complicated trap for us, which would gradually lead us into an illustration from his day's hunting. Roy drew audibly on his corncob, and H. smacked his lips, preparing to pounce from the abstract to the concrete.

"Chance!" he said. "Why, man! If there were any probability in chance, I would have shot a deer today!"

"Did you?" I said.

"No. But I saw one."

"Didn't you shoot?" asked Roy, his pipe forgotten.

"No, I didn't shoot."

"Well, what did you do?"

"I pointed my finger at it!" said H., dramatically. "Now—do you call that chance? Or purpose?"

I hung my rifle muzzle down on a wall peg. "I take it you *intended* to shoot the deer?" I said. "But some purpose from a great exterior stayed your hand, so you pointed your finger instead?"

"Precisely," H. chuckled. "Absolutely."

"Huh," said Roy, dryly. "Buck fever, an' at your age!"

"Indigestion," said I.

These were lame explanations, and besides we felt there was considerable more back of the story than met the ear. Recently H. figured up from old diaries the number of trips he had taken to this country. Counting camping trips, fishing and hunting trips, they totalled eighty! He had been deer hunting thirty different seasons, and his record was impressive. Furthermore, he had never in his life complained of indigestion. He was evidently getting us into a prearranged corner.

"You claim," he went on, "that my experience with the deer this afternoon was an effect, not a cause."

"Sure it was," Roy said, nervous to hear the rest.

"Well, it wasn't," H. said. "It was both. Moreover, all causes can be effects, all effects causes."

Roy turned his wet socks on the rafter so as to dry their other sides. "It's all runnin' off of me like rain off a roof," he protested.

"It's getting pretty swampy, at that," I agreed. "Darn you H., anyway!"

"On the contrary," he continued, taking his own time, "everything becomes quite simple at this point." Here he began to make those marvellously expressive gestures with his hands, lean, squarish, hands which you remember always when you think of H. "I pointed at that deer," he said, "and since you so desire, we'll call my gesture an effect produced by cause or causes unknown. Yet I propose to demonstrate that the effect shall be proved a cause:—you see, it caused me not to shoot that deer, and it causes us now to sit here pondering the subject."

In the face of this, Roy and I cheerfully admitted that black was white and that up was down, depending on the point of view. And we went to our bunks in the shelter of the long brown ridges, little dreaming of the chain of events crawling toward us from the future.

But I *did* dream, just a little. At first I could not get to sleep. The pine boughs sang above the cabin roof, like remote 'cellos. I thought I heard a porcupine prowling in front of the cabin, and an old doe snorted on the ridge toward Killman Pond. I fell to pondering our oblique conversation of a moment before. H.'s pointing his finger at a buck deer *was* unusual. At least he had made it sound so; and I knew he felt it so himself. I set it down as a continuation of the hard luck that had dogged him through the last three deer seasons. I still believed in luck, especially in connection with deer hunting, but I hadn't reached the point of calling it Fate.

Four seasons ago, H. had finished building himself a home. The dining room is dominated by a huge brick fireplace, and even a glance at it warms you. The room is panelled with Pennsylvania chestnut, and the ceiling beams are hand hewn, solid and convincing. Above the fireplace is a rectangle of sacred space, a space where the master of the house would hang his finest oil painting—if he were a sportsman he would hope for a Benson, or a Winslow Homer. But in H.'s house, for some seasons, the space had remained vacant.

"I'll get a buck this fall," he would say. "I'll have it mounted by the finest taxidermist in the world, and I'll hang it there to last me when I'm really old and begin to write a book about myself."

Lying in my bunk, listening to the clumsy maraudings of the porcupine, I remembered H. standing in front of that fireplace and staring at the vacant space above the hewn mantle. One subsequent fall he had stepped on a dead spruce twig, and his buck had got away clean. The November after that, he had come upon an old gray monarch on the slope of Dark Cove Mountain when his glasses were so steamed he couldn't see to shoot. Last season he had seen only does, and this year he had pointed his finger! If my belief in luck were even partly valid, I felt that H. was due for a standing shot at something weighing close to three hundred pounds, with horns to match.

That night in the cabin, when I finally dozed off, I dreamed very dimly of a great-antlered buck in a key-road. Dreams, I have thought, result from some digestive menace, and are nothing upon which to base a prognosis. I had eaten some mince pie of my own devising, which may be reason enough for the fantods. When I awoke, the dream retreated before the more essential fragrance of the coffee pot.

After breakfast, we settled on the day's hunting territory. H. guessed he would hunt the base of the big ridge to the northwest, and Roy decided he would take me over toward the Second Chain burn. We separated long before the sun had melted the white furry frost from the beech leaves underfoot, long before the old gray trunks had taken on form and substance.

Roy is a native guide, and he can concentrate on deer for hours. I can't. Sometimes, looking through the silence at a spruce tree, I see beneath the bark to the wood, see through the wood into its fibrovascular

bundles, see beyond that toward infinite divisibility—
and this fruitless imagining makes me a poor deer hunter. This time I came back to earth at a signal from
Roy. "Sh-h-h! I hear one."

I listened, trembling a little, watching Roy's lynx-
eyes search the thickets. What he heard turned out to
be a carousing red squirrel. Roy knows how to keep a
hunter hunting!

At the edge of the Second Chain burn, we stopped.
This was my only day in camp, and truly I neither deserved nor expected to shoot a deer. I carried a rifle for
the form of the thing, and expected to shoot nothing
but a porcupine or a roosting partridge.

"I'm hungry," I said. It was barely ten o'clock.

"Hungry!" glared Roy. "*Hungry!* You got a gan-
der-gut!"

"Yes."

"Well," he said. "What do you say we work back to
Killman Pond brook?"

"Are you thirsty?" I asked.

"No—I ain't. Just seemed better to eat handy to
water. But I ain't fussy."

So we sat together on a double spruce blowdown and
from our hunting shirt pockets removed two huge
liver sandwiches. They were as thick as sofa pillows. I
took a bite, and began to chew industriously.

Roy, too, was in the middle of a mouthful when his

eyes suddenly turned a shade darker. His jaws stopped working. He braced himself without apparent movement, other than a slight stiffening of his body. "What was that?"

"I didn't hear a thing," I said, my voice muffled by a full mouth.

"I heard a deer!"

Eighty yards away the spruce bushes trembled. I concentrated so intensely on the spot that my eyes watered. Presently the bushes moved again, and a buck stepped into view, stopped with fore-feet braced, head high and magnificently alert. He pranced sideways, placing himself between two small beeches. He was facing me squarely.

"I can see him," I whispered. "Shall I shoot?"

"Yes," Roy whispered.

As I reached down for my rifle, I knocked the liver sandwich off the blowdown. It fell silently, coming apart on the moss. I cuddled the rifle stock against my cheek and drew the ivory bead down fine into the rear sight notch. I squeezed the trigger, holding my breath until I thought my lungs would explode. With the discharge, the rifle jumped in my hands, and the buck vanished into thin air.

"Never touched him," I said.

"You got him," said Roy.

My nostrils twitched at the whiff of powder smoke.

I drew down the lever of my rifle and jacked in another cartridge. Lifting our feet high, like a couple of old cock partridges, we moved cautiously toward where the deer had been standing. He lay stone dead underneath the beech trees, and I don't think he had taken a single step after I fired.

Roy stood looking down at the deer. "I haven't seen a better head come out of the woods in ten seasons," he said. The spikes were unusually long, the horns and points well formed, and not so symmetrical as to be uninteresting. But I was thinking of chance, or luck if you prefer. A woods appetite at ten in the morning had been in charge of things—not a trained stillhunter. It seemed scarcely sporting to have shot a buck as handsome as this after having been in the woods only four hours. H. had been in for two weeks, and I wished he could have been standing in my moccasins. This buck deserved that space above his fireplace.

"Roy," I said, as we lashed the deer to a couple of dry spruce poles, "a fellow with my luck doesn't have much use for brains, does he?"

"No," he replied, unhesitatingly. "You don't even see a buck like this once in five years, let alone a standing shot!" He finished a complicated knot in the lashings and strapped on his belt axe.

"I wish H. had been here. I'd have passed him my rifle, honest I would."

"He wouldn't of took it," Roy said. "He'd ruther you got a deer than to get one himself. That's his way."

"But he's had four years of hard luck."

"His luck'll turn," said Roy. "You mind what I say."

We got the sling poles to our shoulders and toted the deer down along the ridge toward camp. It was two o'clock when we got in. We were pretty well fagged. H. was waiting for us—empty-handed. His eyes danced with delight as he helped us down with the deer. He fingered the horns and counted the points. "Great work! Oh, simply great!" We told our tale, and H. beamed, and I had no heart to ask him about his day on the big ridge to the northwest. He saved me the trouble by saying he hadn't seen hide, hoof, or hair. It didn't seem to bother him in the least. He spoke of the beauty of the long brown ridges, and never mentioned luck. We got a late lunch, and made it a kind of banquet. It was the last day of hunting.

That afternoon Roy stayed in the cabin to pack up, and H. asked me to go with him for the last two hours of daylight. He knew I didn't like to hunt alone. We took a canoe and crossed the lake toward the great ridge beyond which vanishes the sun in Fall. We hauled the canoe into the brush over the seawall, and struck out afoot through the darkling cedars.

There's something sobering about the last afternoon of the last day in camp. There are long-fingered shadows, and a hovering chill which remind you that your freedom here is at an end. A hint of the first big snow loiters in the vault above, and on the deadwaters the black ice lies sinister. Another week, another day, and the forest will be smothered white and lonely—snow, without a man-track on its vastness. You long to stay, but may not. You want to desert, but something mocks you, daring you to stay and try your steel.

I could see H.'s breath puffing white over the shoulder of his faded hunting shirt. I could see the little white circle on the receiver of his rifle, where Roy had wound the sling ring with twine so that it wouldn't jingle. H. tested the wind, looked at his compass, and jacked a cartridge into the chamber of his rifle. He let the hammer down to half-cock, and went on. I followed closely. H. could talk all he wished of cause and effect and Unity. But when a good hunter goes four years without one good chance, he's under the spell of foul fortune.

We struck a key-road, long years abandoned by lumbermen, and turned north by west, up wind. There was ritual in this last short hour of hunting. I felt a faint shame at deserting the tired old forest just when winter was preparing a siege. I can see it all as plain as writing: a winding trail, interrupted by mouldering blowdowns, untracked by human feet. On one side the trail was flanked by a sepulchral cedar swamp extending back to the seawall; on the other by regiments of spruce and beech—the sloping forefoot of Duck Lake Mountain. Deep in here the sun had vanished, challenged and beaten by shadow—all except one urchin shaft of gold which had tunnelled a rift in the cedars. As I watched, the shaft appeared to flicker, and I stopped in my tracks. There was no wind to wave the dead ferns at the edge of the trail where the light had fallen!

H., too, saw the motion. His left hand stiffened toward me, commanding silence. We knelt there on a little knoll, and watched the most magnificent buck step into view. I suddenly remembered my dream of a buck in a key-road, and my scalp prickled. Could I have dreamed this creature into reality? He was near enough for me to count his points and guess a mammoth spread, and he stood so that the shaft of sunlight drew a gold halation around him.

H. brought his rifle to his shoulder, and I waited for the report. Plenty of time—an easy, standing shot of less than sixty yards. My head was inches from H.'s right ear. "Go ahead and shoot!" I whispered.

H. lifted his cheek off the stock, looked long at the buck, and smiled. He brought the rifle into position again, and still the deer didn't know we were there!

"Hurry!" I hissed, as quietly as possible. I was shaking, as Roy expresses it, like a chicken's foot in the mud.

H. was grinning quite broadly, now—and again he had taken the rifle down from firing position. My heart whacked hard against my ribs. I was panicky, then dumbfounded as H. let the hammer down to half cock, deliberately raised his right arm—and *pointed his finger at the buck!*

O vacant place above the chestnut mantel! O chance, O luck, beyond wildest imaginings! Who would have passed it up so serenely, but H.? The buck caught the motion of H.'s arm in a flash. His head jerked toward us, high, startled, fine. We took each a breath-halting swallow of his majesty before he cleared an eight-foot blowdown and was gone, flying his flag in our faces!

"What the devil ails you, H.?" I cried. "You'll never see another like that in a lifetime!"

"It was too far," said H., softly.

"It was an easy shot, and you know it!" I wanted to take off my hat and jump on it.

"I might have missed," said H.

"You *couldn't* have missed!"

"Well," he chuckled, "—I *did!*"

"But, H.! He belonged over your fireplace."

"You know," he said, "I'm not so sure. I think he

belongs right here—where he is. I simply couldn't bear to change the picture of him here. I don't know why. I never will—except that trophies at my age are not so much to brag about, as to remember by. And I'll remember that old fellow, just as we saw him. Never fear."

I understood. All I had to do was look around me at the darker twilight in the cedars, the sky at peace with everything under it, the gray moss bearding the trees with prehistoric gravity, the glow on the lake that lingered rather than depart. This was where the buck with the gold light over him belonged.

But I got a fine taxidermist to mount the head of my buck from the Second Chain burn, and I gave the mount to H. It hangs over his mantel in the dining room.

POP'S DAY OFF

On the ninth of September, in the year of our Lord, 1936, Charles Elmer Thornton, woodsman, took a day off and went pickerel fishing. In the case of Charles Elmer Thornton, hereinafter and by all men known as "Pop," a day off calls for the ringing of chimes, the unfurling of banners, or the explosion of a barrel of Giant powder. Considerable of the last-named is necessary to blast Pop loose from his work. Thus, all of us who have aided and abetted, cozened and cajoled, or tricked and decoyed Pop away from his hewing axe for a few hours, feel like participants in historic matters. Pop works three hundred and sixty-four days a year except for leap years, when it's three-sixty-five.

Pop has been ten years a boy, forty years a woodsman, and three years the superintendent of the Dobsis Club, which is not a club at all, but a cluster of small buildings in a wilderness near the New Brunswick border.

The Dobsis "Club" is owned by H.S.D., the man to

whom this volume is dedicated. H. shares his cabins, his clearing and his salmon stream with certain friends and relatives—but their eyes must first blaze in the approved manner at mention of such words as tracking snow, whitewater, beech ridge, venison, fly rod, settin' pole, wangan, alder swamp, poke logan hole, black growth and a mad practice known as "cruising." H.'s use of cruising is not to be confused with yachting. It means marking a spot on the blue-print map of wilderness-township No. Four, and reaching it on foot through the woods, by the grace of God and a forty-cent compass. One of the motives of cruising is to get lost. Only in this way may one derive the incomparable joy of some time finding his trail back to the Dobsis Club, or Third Chain cabin.

One of the former owners of the Dobsis Club caused a flagpole to be erected. In 1934, years after H. came into possession, he, Pop Thornton and I held a meeting to decide whether or not the flagpole was a mark of ostentation in the wild lands. There was no smiling or buffoonery as we cast our written ballots in an old butter crock. H. counted all three of them, and announced that the flagpole was doomed. Pop and I cut it down. Throughout the deer season, we burned it chunk by chunk in the ancient Wood & Bishop stove, and by its warmth we dried our moccasins and exaggerated old memories.

The event was not without a certain melancholy. The flagpole had been such a venerable part of the scene. As you looked across the stream toward Dark Cove Mountain, it had always drawn its clean white margin down the picture. So my conscience yawned in its sleep, as if I had discovered too late a tendency to vandalism. "I bet we'll miss that flagpole some day," I said to H.

"Bet we won't," H. growled. "It never belonged here."

But on the ninth of September, 1936, I missed it badly. I felt it was needed for a ceremony substantial enough to signalize Pop Thornton's day off. We could have run up a satchel of Pop's edged tools—just to get them out of his reach for a while. Or we might have flown his sacred hewing axe at half mast. Now, with the flagpole gone, I am obliged to write the episode, rather than honor it.

Pop Thornton is fifty-three, six feet one, and he balances the granary scales at one fifty-nine. Although he delights in still-hunting, woods cruising, and his patented method of catching pickerel, his first love is tools. I do not believe that Pop would abandon his family for a double-bitted axe, but the idea comes to mind when you see him pick up, admire, and finally go to work with that implement. He cherishes his drills, augers, gimlets, spoke-shaves, bark-spuds, planes and adzes. But he simply cannot stay away from axes.

A hewing axe, perfectly offset, fearfully edged, with a slender, whippy handle, will make the whites of Pop's eyes show. "I could take that, an' hew a sill so you'd think 'twas planed." He is not boasting. He is stating a fact and honoring an edged tool.

Pop's face is of the type known as lantern-jawed. From hair line to jaw point, he is one axe-helve long. When he smiles, which is often, the corners of his mouth vanish at the lobes of his ears—and his ears are set at an angle which is advantageous in a fair wind.

One summer, by trailing Pop around with a thermometer, I was successful in getting him to go swimming in the lake. It was 109° in the shade. He protested violently that he had to make a new weathervane for the club house, and did not consent until I had stirred the mercury to a blistering 132° by the judicious application of a hot pipe bowl.

The swim gave me a chance to observe Pop's build. Take an elongated human skeleton, and fill the chest cavity with a heart as big as a steamboat boiler. Cement it there with a gallon of drollery, and add one spacious imagination. Stretch a raw hide over the whole, set it in the hot sun so it will shrink tightly over the bones, and you have Pop. But I see I have left out a whetstone.

Pop's heart is as tender as the rest of him is tough. Every year on the place he grows a beef critter, whose earliest known maternal ancestor came up over the ice from Grand Lake Stream sixty-five years ago. Pop is heartbroken at the annual necessity of butchering the critter. Invariably he threatens to call in "someone that ain't met my yearlin' before."

Pop's kitchen is a haven for cats. They have kittens there under the stove. If you should be invited to eat with the family, you will wade through the sleeping forms of hounds to your chair at the kitchen table. Even a mouse is assured of warmth, food and a nest. But there's bound to be one exception to such hospitality, otherwise Pop would be inhuman. The exception is a fiend named William Conroy Gains. In 1923, Billy Gains borrowed Pop's favorite hewing axe and returned it a month later with a nick in the blade as large as a slice of melon. There is no doubt in Pop's mind, and but a shadow in my own, that the soul of William Conroy Gains will ultimately be received in Hell.

Billy Gains ravaged Pop's axe all of thirteen years ago, but he remains as hot and virulent a sinner as if it had happened yesterday. In Dobsis' recent tradition, all things vile and contemptible are likened to Billy Gains. He is the apex of degradation. In a word, he is the man who nicked Pop's hewing axe, and silently stole away.

In 1935 when we were in hunting, Pop entered the club house, rammed a chunk of yellow birch into the stove, and said: "I cut, split an' piled two cord an' a half of wood today. Workin' in mighty skimpsy timber, too."

"Honest, Pop, did you?"

"Yes, sir. By the yantin' Moses, I done it. You know *how* I done it? I got to thinkin' of Billy Gains, an' what he done to my axe that time. An' bime by, every time I took a clout with my axe I got to thinkin' it was Billy I was cloutin'. I'd cut two cord an' a half before the 'joyment run out!"

The next September, a few days before Pop's day off, he told us of another and more disastrous revenge he had taken on Billy. Pop had been dreaming that he was fishing through the ice, side by side with his enemy. Any dream involving Billy Gains is a nightmare, but this one was worse. Billy caught all the fish —three big lake trout, a landlocked salmon, and a pickerel—and his tipups not ten yards from Pop's.

Awaking early in the after-misery of the dream, Pop went moaning out into the kitchen to build the morning fire. His wife, Katherine, had left some bread to rise in the warming oven, and while building the fire, Pop set the dough carefully on the kitchen table out of harm's way. But in the dim light, the pale, vapid appearance of the nicely rounded dough suggested Billy Gains' face. Shivering in his long underwear, Pop's lip curled. In his own words, this is what happened: "I says to the dough: 'Pie Face! Ole Pie Face Billy Gains! You'd nick my hewin' axe, would you?' I says. More I looked, more I seen the likeness between the dough an' Billy's face. First thing I knowed, I'd smacked Katherine's dough with the whole bigness of my hand! *Whuff!* An' the dough mashed out same as pie crust. I don't know but flatter, even! Katherine like to fainted dead away when she seen it, an' I had to tell her two stove lids had fell on it. Katherine says, 'Well, I never *heard* 'em fall!' An' so I says to her, 'Course you didn't! They fell on the dough an' got mufflered.' "

It was a day or two after hearing of this domestic apocalypse, that C.F.S., Jr., our guide Harley, and I, began working on Pop to get him loose for a day's pickerel fishing. It usually takes about a week to nail him on the line, and we were late in laying the ground work, which accounts for our use of foul play. We had taken a few fine trout from Killman Pond, but hadn't been able to raise a landlocked salmon. Pickerel were coming great in the wide mouth of Wabassas Stream, and we had had a field day with yellow bucktail flies, and plug casting with a Pikie Minnow. Each evening, when we returned, we would all file out to Pop's work shop and coax him. He wouldn't give an inch of ground. Pickerelin'? Should *say* not! No time for nothing at all, let alone pickerelin'. Two old does an' a spike horn had busted into the garden an' wrecked it, and the fence had to be re-builded. Had to take the shaft out of the boat an' re-pack it. Had to steam out some new ribs for the eighteen-footer I had busted in the quick water on Fourth Machias Stream. Pickerelin'? Huh! The moon warn't right. An' besides, who'd keep the dogs out'n the porkypines if Pop went fishin'? An' re-nail the shingles on the shed roof, an'—"Every time my back is turned, somethin' turrible happens that I don't do, only I just repair it afterwards."

"Well, anyway," C.F.S., Jr. said, after an unavailing session one evening, "Katherine said for us to tell you supper was ready, and please come right away."

Pop drew his spoke shave down the length of a dry spruce he was shaping into a setting pole. Coming to the end of the pole, he set the spoke shave aside, made a tormented motion with his arm, and cried: "By God! You tell Katherine—for *me!*—that I ain't got no time to eat for two or three days, at *least!* Tell her I got the glue an' flatiron all hot to patch a canoe. Tell her—no! Tell her, for good an' all, that I ain't never goin' to bother eatin' again. Too much to do."

I said: "Tomorrow's our last day in camp. Come on, go with us. Pickerel are coming great. You're too thin, Pop. You need a good feed of pickerel."

"Ain't I just said how I'm all done with eatin' for

good? Besides, pickerel ain't fit to eat unless they're right fresh out of the water."

"Harley and I'll get the cook outfit together," C.F.S., Jr. said. "We'll all cook supper on the beach at the mouth of the stream tomorrow evening—last night in camp, Pop. What do you say?"

It was a hot, muggy evening, and Harley fanned Pop's brow with a two months old *Bangor Daily News*. Pop wiped his forehead with the back of his wrist. "Too danged much on my mind," he sighed.

C.F.S., Jr. turned to me. "Trouble is, Pop's afraid he'll get skunked."

Pop waved the *Bangor News* away, and machined an expression of belligerence. "Hah! So I can't catch pickerel, can't I? How about that time a year ago— last day off I had—over on Second Chain deadwater?" He looked at me for corroboration.

"Just luck, it was," I told him, shaking my head. "I know plenty of fellows that can really *catch* pickerel. Fellows that don't depend on good luck, or the way the moon is."

"Who, for instance?" Pop growled. "Not *you!*"

"I didn't say me. I'm supposed to be an expert, and can't catch many."

Pop leaned forward, his hand groping apparently in hope of closing on some such blunt instrument as a cantdog handle. "Well, *who*, then?" he challenged.

[113]

"Billy Gains!" I said, and took for the woods beyond the clearing.

We got started the next day shortly after lunch. Skirting the shore of Compass Lake in two canoes, we headed for the mouth of Wabassas Stream, six miles away. C.F.S., Jr. and Harley were in the lead canoe. Pop and I trailed. I was privileged to act as his guide for the day. Once out of sight of his work, the vacation spirit crept into Pop. He leaned against the bow thwart and sighed with prodigious contentment. I had rigged my plug casting rod for him, and when we reached the mouth of the stream, he picked it up gingerly, seated himself on the bow thwart, and began casting. I could see the faded blue back of his denim shirt, and darker crossed streaks where his suspenders had once shaded the material. There is something permanent and steadfast about Pop's back. It's like a weathered ledge.

Suddenly we heard Harley and C.F.S., Jr. talking excitedly. We saw their canoe on the far side of the stream, and astern of them a commotion in the water. "Oh, dang it all, anyways," groaned Pop, with carefully invented dismay, "they got one a'ready!" A mark of Pop's humor is that vituperation indicates congratulation, criticism means satisfaction, and all groaning expresses contentment.

"Sure they've got one," I said.

"One less for me to ketch," he sighed. Then he cast, and got a backlash. He looked at me as if I had deliberately planned it, cleared his reel and cast again. The second cast was so fine as to astonish Pop, who had little patience with this method of fishing. Beginning the retrieve, he observed: "You never made a cast as good as that in your life."

"That's right."

Disappointed at arousing no spark, Pop tried again: "What I always say is, I can do anything with practice."

"You bet," I said, not yet daring to disagree.

"And better than you, too," he persisted, hopefully. Pop loves to start small, bright rebellions. Many have been our embattled arguments on fishing, horseshoe pitching and whether or not the world is flat. "I am an authority," asserted Pop, after a moment, "on pratickly everything."

He was about midway of his retrieve when he said this, and as if to corroborate him, a swirl appeared beneath his incoming Pikie Minnow lure. Spotting it from the corner of his eye, Pop lurched and hooked the fish—a pickerel of about nineteen inches. He nodded by way of stamping his last statement with his own approval and kept reeling. When the fish came close, he reached overside and with his clawlike hand, got the pickerel by the scruff of the neck and hoisted him aboard. From his pocket he removed a large bone handled knife, and tapped the fish once, emphasizing the *coup de grâce* with a grunt.

From the cook outfit behind the stern seat I got out a bottle of cold ale and passed it forward, opened. Pop applied the bottle to his lips, and his arrow-shaped Adam's apple bobbed twice. He set the bottle aside and looked all around at the sky where some big white clouds were dozing along. I began to look around, too —at everything.

Away up a bald eagle soared on still, wide wings. Pop was looking at the eagle, too.

"Bet he's got a seven-foot spread," I said.

"Six and a half," corrected Pop, after a moment's study. "A dollar."

"How are we going to prove it?"

"We ain't goin' to," he said. "That's the way to bet. No one can't lose."

Shoreward among the water-killed stumps, a heron perched motionless on one leg, and some redwing blackbirds made music in the reeds. C.F.S., Jr. and Harley, small in the distance, shouted with renewed delight as they landed a second pickerel. Pop turned around. The grin on his face was like a wave in the sunlight. "You know," he said, "I ain't been as happy, nor I ain't felt as good, not since the night I dreamed Billy Gains fell out of an airplane an' come down a-straddle of a fence with iron pickets. I feel so dang good it mighty near hurts—only for just one little thing—" He hesitated, and his expression turned to one of acute, apologetic misery.

"This is your day off," I told him, genuinely troubled by his cloud of woe. "Tell me what's wrong, Pop. If there's anything I can do, you tell me, and I'll do it. Didn't you send me those canoe poles last Christmas?"

"It's about fishin'," Pop replied, solemnly.

"Oh—then take my fly rod, if you'd rather. There's some big bucktails in my fly book. Or—"

"It goes a good deal deeper'n that. You're an expert —that is, you claim to be one—"

"I don't either!"

"Well, you write like you *thought* you was one then, anyway. Point is, I want to fish my way. The way I allus fished as a boy."

"Good gosh. Fish any way you like, Pop."

"Sure you won't mind?"

" 'Course not. What if I did?"

Pop took a long gulp from the ale bottle and held it to the sun to measure the remainder. "Well," he said, decisively, "that gives me stren'th an' forty-tude."

And forthwith he removed from his shirt a shaped white pine block over which was wound, if my eyes did not deceive me, about sixty yards of nine-thread cuttyhunk which had lately been introduced to a tar barrel. To the end of the line was attached the ancient and honorable market fisherman's pickerel lure—a Buhl spinner.

Pop held up his gear and said: "There she is. Look at her!" The pickerel he had just caught gave a flop on the floor of the canoe. Pop gave the fish a truculent look and said: "Be still, there." Then he took from a tobacco can two strips of pork rind about two inches long, and tapered. These he fastened to two of the points of the treble hook. He swung the lure gently back and forth, admiring it.

"Now, I couldn't be no more peaceful and contented than if Billy Gains was layin' on a red ant hill, tied thar, an' me sprinklin' molasses on the top of him, an' a swarm of yellow-tailed hornets just gettin' the wind of him."

Then Pop began to whirl the spinner violently and horizontally around his head, the coiled line in the bottom of the canoe in front of him. He took no particular aim. The big idea was distance. The farther the cast, the finer the cast. Wherever the spinner struck the water was the exact spot at which he claimed to have been shooting all along. "If you can't get bull's eyes," he explained, "just take an' move 'em over into the path of the bullit. That's how I come to be sech a perfect shot."

After a few preliminary casts, I observed Pop looking at a rock about a hundred feet distant in mid-stream. He began spinning, working up gradually to an estimated thousand r.p.m., or until the spinner resembled a silver halo around his battered hat. When he let fly, the spinner shot off at an angle some forty degrees east of the rock. The spinner was still travelling like a bullet, about ten feet over a tangle of dead, dry shoregrowth, when the end of the line was reached. The wood block twitched in Pop's pocket, the line stretched, contracted, and jerked the spinner safely back into open water at the exact base of a cedar stump in the center of some sparse lily pads. "Boy! Just perfect! Did you see me hit that stump?"

"It was a beauty," I acknowledged.

He began the retrieve. Pop's handline retrieve is well worth learning: you let the line run through your left hand, and coil at your feet. With your right hand, you sort of rake it in by means of a long, violent arm motion. Spinner and pork rind together have an action fatal to pickerel. Pop advocates a sincere grunt with each pull of the right arm. Thus his retrieve has sound, as well as form and action. It goes: "Ah-*unh* . . . Ah-*unh* . . . Ah-*unh*. . . ."

On this preposterous cast, after the fourth or fifth grunt, something hit deep under water. Pop's arm stopped in mid-sweep. His eyebrows, arching in excitement and surprise, pushed his hat an inch farther back on his forehead. He was fast to a fish, the size of which is locally measured as "paddle blade."

Sometimes the line moved sideways through the water, swift as only a pickerel can take it. Then it moved not at all, then it moved toward us as Pop tugged and hauled. I kept turning the canoe so that Pop might handle his fish from the proper angle. C.F.S., Jr. and Harley had come close, unnoticed, and their sudden whooping added to the general confusion. Pop had begun addressing the invisible pickerel in valiant terms.

The floor of the canoe was a chaos of coiled, tar-treated line, which had fouled several loose bass plugs, plucking them like dissolute and predatory fruit from the gunwales where I had so neatly hung them. The tip of my favorite casting rod, and the reel at the butt of my sacred Leonard fly rod were lashing about, the victims of unexpected pressures and writhings. At some point the handle of a frying pan entered the engagement, setting up a clangor that echoed mildly from the steep, rocky shore across the stream. The blue heron, terror-struck, took wing after several futile attempts, and a flock of black duck, disturbed at their feeding nearly half a mile away, made a neat dark V in the coloring afternoon sky.

C.F.S., Jr. and Harley circled around us, shouting: "Snub him, Pop! Take a half hitch somewhere!"

By the quickening zig-zags of the line, I saw that the fish was in close. He came to the surface and gave what Pop calls "a larrup." A larrup is a doubling, writhing, tail-thrashing twist, on or near the surface of the water. The pickerel threw a fine sheet of spray for ten feet in all directions, and sounded. I think, when he saw the fish closely, that you could have snared Pop's eyes with a boom chain. His final "ah-*unh!*" came from the depths of his soul. A twenty-four inch pickerel, chunky-built, came clear of the water, swung toward us across the canoe, backward to the other side, out over the water on four feet of line. Pop turned completely around in the process, winding himself hopelessly in the litter on the canoe bottom.

Directly over the canoe, on the start of the second backswing, the hooks came free. The fish plopped into mid-tangle, and Pop pounced on him—all fours. If we hadn't been in one of Bill Sprague's nineteen-foot canoes, we'd have upset. Pop finally got a firm hold on the fish, and administered the last rite with an alder stick that served as an extension handle for the frying pan. Next he looked at me, and cried: "Head for shore. We'll have this one fresh. Head straight in— not on a slant. He might spoil on us if you go on a slant!"

Our meal that night was both a triumph and a climax. Bulging with pride and glory, Pop was easily the hero of his own day off—which is exactly as it should be. He made a fetish of getting his fish into the frying pan in a minimum number of seconds after it was caught. With one rake of his hard-shelled hand, he tore off the limbs of a dead cedar and touched a match to them. Into the pan went the bacon fat. Ever and anon, his brows wrinkled with calculated worry, Pop would draw out his two-pound watch and check the time. Harley dressed the pickerel and sliced him into appropriate pieces. The grease began to smoke. Pop got out his watch again. He dropped a chunk of pickerel into the pan. It hissed. "Three minutes an' twenty-two seconds," he said. "I guess it's fresh enough."

Ten miles from the nearest human being not of our own crew, we ate supper in the still twilight. The smoke went crawling away—bluish against the darkening spruces. Boiling in the big kettle were a dozen ears of sweet corn Pop had salvaged from his garden. The remaining chunks of pickerel browned in the pan. Tea steeped to one side of the fire—black, dynamic, Maine tea. On a table Pop had constructed of split cedar, rested one of Katherine's lemon pies—the pride of Washington County. The filling of these pies is neither hard, like rubber, nor gelatinous, like guava jelly. It runs smooth and hot, and tastes of real lemons imported from Bangor, and even a small man can devour a whole one.

We arranged Pop at a comfortable angle, and waited on him by turns, competing to obey his momentous orders first.

"More pickerel, please. I'm hungry. I could eat a boiled skull stuffed with bugs." More pickerel appeared to his hand.

"Now the butter for my corn," he commanded, a gaunt king enthroned on a rock on the shore of Wabassas stream. "Just a small piece—about as big as a horse's upper lip from his eye down."

The last word is Pop Thornton's. With his axeman's hands, he rolled a cigarette as nimbly as a sleight of hand artist. He lit the cigarette with an ember which C.F.S., Jr. brought him from the fire. He lay back, puffing, the cigarette at an angle, his hands locked underneath his head. "Boy," he sighed. "I'm happy. I never felt so good—upon my soul to God, never. I'm a mind—danged if I ain't a mind to track down Billy Gains an' give him my other hewin' axe, just for a present."

CHRISTMAS FOR TWO

"Look out, Dad!" Through the network of brown November branches I could see into the little open where my father watched for the driven grouse. This was the shot he loved best in all bird shooting. He had taught me its strategy when I was twelve, taught me right here in the old Atkinson cover.

He stood alert and calm, feet close together, gun forward in position of easy readiness, his left hand well out under the barrels. Then he saw the bird, and the gun moved in that clean, smooth swing for which he was noted. But this time, part way through the motion, there was a jerk of uncertain co-ordination. He fired twice, and kept turning away from me as he followed the bird's flight. He had missed again!

Stiffly, as though his legs hurt, he walked to an old apple tree and leaned against it. I scrambled over the stone wall and broke through the blackberry briars that separated us. Dad smiled. He opened his gun and removed the smoking shells—but he did not reload.

"It's my legs, Jimmy. They're tired—dead tired. They ache."

"But, Dad——"

The wind stirred a lock of silver-white hair that curled below his hatbrim: "Don't get excited. It's nothing but what most old fellows get. It's rheumatism."

This tall, fine-eyed man to whom I belonged; who had taught me grouse and wildfowl shooting; who had held my wrist while I caught my first trout; who had taught me to *walk;* this man—my father—was suddenly gone old before me, white-haired, sunken-cheeked, and seventy! "Why—*Dad!*"

He leaned heavily on a low limb, taking the weight off his legs. "Hush-hush, now. It's nothing at all."

I had to help him home. He wouldn't go the short cut—afraid someone would see him leaning on me, or see the muscles of his face drawn taut with pain. We went by Blanchard's wood road and up Hickory Lane along the marshes. The only person we saw was one of the Tibido children, a hungry, tousle-headed urchin of seven—*barefooted*, the first of November!

Dad never let on he had seen the child until I got him home and into his chair. Then he said: "I'm afraid we won't be able to do much for the Tibidos this Christmas."

Already Dad had begun to think of that!

I can remember as many as thirty of us around the long dinner table: Grandfather always carved the game which Dad and my older brothers had shot for the occasion. Grandfather would say: "Henry (that's Dad), is this knife as sharp as you can get it?" Dad would say "Yes, sir," but grandfather would pick up the steel and whet away for five minutes while our mouths watered. "There now, I guess we're ready," he'd finally remark, and plunge the knife into the breast of the roast goose or black duck, peering critically at the issuing juices to determine if the bird were properly done. Invariably it was. So grandfather would part his whiskers with practiced accuracy and say: "A-h-h-h!" and of course the womenfolk would all congratulate one another on their cooking.

Cranberry sauce, four vegetables, a sideboard creaking under its burden of assorted pies, cakes, fruits— and cider pitchers.

At Christmas dinner, the pièce de résistance was game—traditionally shot by members of the Osborn family. But the real ceremony, the welding of the Christmas spirit, came on Christmas Eve. That was Mother's. Every year she went down to the Tibido's shanty laden with baskets of food, the rest of us following with presents for the children. The Tibido children worshiped Mother. She gave because she loved to give, and they knew it.

After supper, at home, we sang *Hark, the Herald Angels, Holy Night,* and *Little Town of Bethlehem* —accompanied by Uncle Alden on the melodeon. Then we gathered by the fire while Mother read Dickens' *Christmas Carol* aloud. That was the final rite, and it seemed to bind us all inseparably.

She read by candlelight, and by the glow from the fire—tipping the book just a trifle to catch its light. Invariably she began with the same words, spoken in the same reverent voice: "Well, children—this is 'A Christmas Carol,' by Charles Dickens." Mother had read that moving masterpiece each Christmas since I was old enough to listen. I think I could recite it all from memory.

Firelight! Marley's ghost rattling its chains while children listened in wide-eyed wonder. Once Uncle Alden went to sleep and snored. And once grandfather became so enraged over Scrooge's stinginess that he rose from his chair, thumping with his cane, and growling through his whiskers, "I'll pound that fellow to a pulp!" Nearly everyone was moist-eyed with sympathy for Bob Cratchit and Tiny Tim. You would see a handkerchief whisking upward now and then. On the rug, as close to the fire as they could get, slept our three fox hounds—Moby, Belle, and Trailer. They twitched, concerned only with their dreams of primitive triumphs.

Most of all, I remember the expression in my father's eyes. This was his day of days. I can only guess at his deep, inarticulate happiness. Under those smoky, hand-hewn beams his family had grown, branched, and matured. Devotion to its meaning, and gratitude for its unity and goodness, overflowed his heart and shone from the depths of his eyes. The Christmas Eve reunion was, I think, a reward for his renowned generosity.

Then, bit by bit, the reward diminished. First the War, and my two brothers lost. My sisters married and moved away. One by one the rooms were vacated, rooms from which for generations we had watched the seasons ebb and flow. Then Mother died—and this was to be our first Christmas without her.

The Tibido urchin had reminded Dad too abruptly of this. I could almost feel the hurt of his thoughts: the Osborn tradition washed up. Nothing left but an album full of tintypes, a basket of last year's tree decorations, and a sheaf of newspaper clippings describing the liquidation of the Osborn cordage business. One of those clippings said: HENRY OSBORN TO SETTLE ONE HUNDRED CENTS ON THE DOLLAR. Dad did. He *would*. It left him almost nothing.

"No," I said to him now, "guess we can't help the Tibidos this year." Impetuously, I added: "Why don't you sell the old place? It's too big for us—now."

He looked at me with a slow far-away smile. The tiny wrinkles gathered at the corners of his eyes. "No, we can fill it Jimmy."

For days I could hear his voice saying that. Then the sound dimmed in the harsh practical clatter of my young and struggling business. By the 23rd of December I had forgotten what Dad said. I shouldn't have, for it was evidence of the strange hope within him. On the night of the 23rd I bought a dressed turkey from the market, and subsequently worked late in my office over a stack of bungled invoices. I bought that turkey because a submerged intuition hinted that a Christmas dinner of wild game—for Dad and me, alone—would be like salting a wound. I went home late, feeling pretty grim.

In the inky dark of the front hall I stumbled over something, and switched on the light. There, arranged with patience and precision, was my duck hunting outfit. Not a detail was lacking, because it was laid out by an old master. Two dozen black duck decoys, tarred lines neatly wound and tied, anchor weights in perfect shape; hat, gunning coat, sweater, boots, and gloves; Uncle Alden's historic old double gun; a box of chilled sixes; my duck call; a water bottle and box of sandwiches; row locks and oars—everything. On the table was the boathouse key, and under the key a note:

Be sure to hunt down all cripples. Lead 'em plenty.

Don't use the duck call too much. Set out at Brick Oven Creek—and bring home the Osborn Christmas dinner! Good luck and good night. Your father.

Oh, time-honored advice—and between its matter-of-fact lines, my father's hunger to carry on a tradition through me! It wrung my heart. The first thing I did was to hide that turkey in the cold shed. If Brick Oven Creek failed to produce, I could always re-discover the turkey. But my prayers to the red gods were for black duck.

Morning on the marsh: A thin arm of red reached down the East, a shaft in a lead-gray sky. Gulls wheeled in, a warning from the open sea. Crows pitched and tumbled in the gusts. The ragged waves followed fast upon each other, and all of them bared their teeth in the salt wind which stung my eyelids.

Ghostly to be sitting there in the old blind at the mouth of Brick Oven! Forty years ago Dad's two brothers had built it of cedar stakes, wire, and marsh thatch. Here, with the very gun I hugged across my chest, Uncle Alden had brought down three geese. Uncle Jim, for whom I was named, had rowed home from this blind with a mixed bag about which, after thirty years, the natives still speak. I had shot my first duck from this very set-out, father beside me to temper my ten-year-old excitement.

Abruptly now, through the swirling snowflakes, five blacks whipped down, their feet braced and wings set to the wind for landing. They nearly caught me reminiscing, but I dropped the farthest one and that gave me time to swing onto the nearest one as he flared. I doubled.

By the time I had pulled the grab from the mud flat and launched the skiff, the down birds had vanished. Wind and snow made a bad business of retrieving. I ought to get a spaniel. When I located the birds, I was about half lost. I knew the wind direction, but had to guess at the angle back to the creek mouth. It was blind rowing, the snow thick and stinging. I never felt more lonely in my life, but I got back, bringing the foundation of the Osborn Christmas dinner. Two fat redlegs —northern blacks, down from the sub-arctic.

I cannot explain the scarcity of ducks that day of traditional duck hunters' weather—wind, cold, snow. Perhaps the birds had taken refuge in the fresh water ponds, inland. Once I started up, trembling to the call of wild geese, a big flock lost in the whirlpools of the sky. But I never saw them, and their weird, forlorn honking grew inaudible as they searched for haven.

At two o'clock, as the abnormally high tide started to ebb, I got another chance. Low to the water, a redleg came racing straight down the creek, the gale on his beam. My first barrel was ten feet over him. The sec-

ond connected while the bird was almost stationary, beating back against the wind.

My last chance was the one which got me into trouble. A pair whistled over from behind me—just luck that I saw them at all. I got one of them by remembering to hold well under. The bird crumpled, but from then on the snow swallowed it. I merely guessed as to where it struck the water. Four birds, past three o'clock, and getting dark fast. Marking the direction of the fallen bird, I hastily took in the set, tossed the blocks into the skiff, and shoved off.

I rowed steadily for ten minutes, counting myself lucky to find the bird. Then, in my mind, I fumbled for the direction home, and I felt as if I were the last man on earth. I couldn't see thirty yards in any direction, and the weird curlicues in the water overside told of a raging tide rip. That, added to ten minutes hard rowing and a northeast gale—all moving in the same direction—had me bewildered on the matter of distance. I guessed myself over a mile from the Brick Oven blind and pulled cross-tide for shore. I figured to make land between Martin's Slough and the Town Bridge and pulled for an hour until it was black dark. You couldn't tell whether you were two yards or two miles from shore.

I stopped rowing and listened, but I could hear nothing above the wind. It was like being marooned on a cloud at midnight, and on every hand I felt the turbulence of the sky. I was properly scared when, suddenly, an oar touched bottom, and an instant later the boat beached violently.

I didn't have the faintest notion where I was, and this taught me something about being lost. You can plant your feet on ground you've trod since boyhood— and you won't recognize it! I saw a light, and after hauling up the skiff, picked up my four birds and headed toward it uncertainly. I was pretty well fagged, dazed by the wind, my face like chilled putty. I actually knocked on the door of that lighted house before I recognized it—the Tibido's poverty-stricken home! I was two miles off course!

From inside an excited child's voice cried out at my knock, her irony all unwitting: "It's Santy Claus! Santy Claus! Oh, mother! Open the door quick!"

Mrs. Tibido opened the door and I stumbled into the close warmth of the little kitchen. For speaking purposes my lips were useless, but I managed a gum-rubber smile for the circle of rapt expectant faces, young and old. Mrs. Tibido wiped her hands on her apron, and offered me one of them. I took the thin fingers in mine.

"We knew you'd come!" she said, happily. "All day the children have been expecting you, Mr. Jimmy."

"Merry Christmas," I mumbled.

That rather broke the ice, and the children rallied around tugging at me and begging me to come and see their Christmas tree. It would have cut you like a rusty knife! A spruce bush stuck in a cracked flower pot with white grocer's twine doing double duty as tinsel and snow. I shook some real snow off my hat onto the "tree." It glistened briefly, and the children's eyes danced.

You know what I did, of course. It was an impulse, I suppose—but it was a Christmas impulse. Anyone would have done the same thing. And it *did* add its mite toward perpetuating a tradition that mankind holds sacred—I mean the Christmas tradition. I left the four black ducks behind me, and went my weary way homeward! The Tibidos totaled seven, counting their mauled kitten. The four ducks would assure them all of plenty. And Dad and I could have the turkey I had hidden in the cold shed. It was a fine plump turkey, and even though it wasn't bagged by one of the two remaining Osborns it would taste good to them. I made a rather bad job of whistling through chapped lips.

Dad was out somewhere when I got home, so I took a hot shower and gradually came back to life. I shaved and dressed and got downstairs just as Dad came in the front door. He was leaning heavily on his cane, but the eagerness in his eyes was jovially apparent. He wanted to know all about my duck hunt.

"Come on," he insisted. "Out with it!"

I described each detail, each bird, the look and feel and smell of the marsh. I told him of getting lost in the storm. He was thirsty for every last drop of description. He sat gazing into the fire, his lips wrinkling with his own reminiscences. "Good!" he said, quietly. "It's good for a man to come face to face with the elements. It gives him respect for them, and for himself. Let's see the ducks."

I had been so long expecting that demand, that when the words actually came, I almost dodged. Just how could I explain the missing ducks, the even graver matter of the forbidden turkey in the cold shed—in the face of my father's intense eagerness?

"Well, Dad," I started, haltingly, "I bought a turkey yesterday. But when I got home late last night to find you had laid out my shooting gear, I knew you'd rather it was black ducks—for old time's sake, shot by an Osborn. So I hid the turkey, Dad—like a thief hiding loot. Then, tonight, when I saw the Tibidos, and the kids' Christmas tree, something got hold of me. I —I thought of Mother, and you, and other Christmases, and they all lumped together inside of me. But —anyway, we've got that turkey, Dad."

It was a solemn moment for me, that Christmas Eve.

So when father started to chuckle, then burst abruptly into laughter, I was a little confused and disturbed. But I think he divested himself of fifteen years during that laugh, the first truly good one I had heard from him since Mother's death. It came right from the deep part of him.

He got his cane, and, still chuckling, went to the sideboard for the decanter and two small glasses. He filled the glasses and handed me one, lifting his own to his lips: "Here's to our Christmas, and to the Tibido's Christmas. They've got the ducks—*and* the turkey! God bless them, every one!"

"What turkey?" I asked, stupidly.

"*The* turkey! I was rummaging in the cold shed this morning, and found it. I've just come from the Tibido's now. I gave it to them!"

"But they wouldn't take *both*," I cried, half angrily.

"Of course they wouldn't. They didn't know. And I didn't know you gave them the ducks—not until after I'd given them the basket. I had wrapped the turkey so they couldn't tell what it was, just as Mother always did."

"Oh, Dad! If Mother were only here to share this with us!" I said, and I could have bitten out my tongue! Dad just nodded. He was thinking, too, that it was the sort of thing she'd appreciate.

That Christmas Eve had a kind of solemn splendor to it. Father and I were happy in a strange, moving way. The evening had a rare quality which makes your heart glad, and makes your throat hurt, too. Mine was glad when Dad said: "We'll have ham and eggs for Christmas dinner. In this instance, finer even than turkey or black duck!" And my throat hurt when, after lighting the candles, he sat in Mother's chair by the fire; when he reached up and took the book from the wall cupboard; when he opened it, leaning just a trifle to catch the light; when he looked up once at the emptiness of the great room, at the smoky hand-hewn beams, and at the memories that dwelt forever in those shadows. My throat hurt unbearably when he looked into the fire, and began: "Well, children— Jimmy—this is *A Christmas Carol*, by Charles Dickens. . . ."

VANCOUVER ISLAND: AN
INSULAR REPORT

I BELIEVE that a man is entitled to conceal from his fellows certain of those things which have fallen dismally short of his original hopes. Random examples might include the weight of trout, first poems, four-flushes after the draw and early love letters. But when a man has an experience which transcends his powers of expression, silence is more than a mere right. It is a public obligation.

In the latter category I had placed my Vancouver Island adventures. It seemed impossible for me to do them justice in words. Accordingly I had consigned the whole affair to the limbo of silence—when I ran across a bloodless little volume entitled: *Vancouver Island: An Insular Report*. It was written by a man named Simeon A. Pottidge. Without malice, I wish to submit that Mr. Pottidge did not understand his theme. His book contains a body of carefully tabulated statistics, and they are probably accurate, but I hold that no one—not even Mr. Pottidge—can describe Olympus, or the Garden of Eden, on a Burroughs adding machine.

For example, on page one, he states: *"Vancouver Island lies sixty miles off the West coast of British Columbia, Canada, Latitude, 49°, Longitude, 125°."*

To me, a very important thing about these lines is that they cross in the island's Alberni district, noteworthy for steelhead, salmon and trout. I would like to add a brief note on my journey in reaching Lat. 49, Long. 125.

I stood under the drab roofs of Bonaventure Station, Montreal. A porter named Jimmy Nicholas had placed my rods and baggage aboard the Transcontinental Limited. It was late December, and my breath steamed. Walking slowly beside the groomed train, I studied the names of the cars, and felt the spirit of the twilight frontier. Fort Nipigon, Fort Dunvegan, Coronation Gulf, Aklavik, Wintring River. Beside these, the names of the dear old Boston & Albany sleepers struck me as unimaginative. "Rosemere" is no match for "Coronation Gulf," nor "Flatbush" for "Wintring River." Then Jimmy Nicholas waved his rubber-matted step at me and told me I had better board her.

Morning: Quebec was gone, and we had begun eating miles from Ontario. I saw my first Hudson's Bay Post in years—a tiny gray-white cluster of buildings whose origin dates to 1670 when Charles II granted one of the most romantic charters in history: "To the Governor and Company of Gentleman Adventurers Trading into Hudson's Bay."

A light snow was falling on the spruce wilderness, on infrequent squaw-blanket and dog-team settlements, on a tall man with a rifle walking into the bush on snowshoes. I wished fleetingly that I might be the boy in the fur cap west of Foleyette who was driving a dog team in tandem harness across a frozen lake. He appeared disgruntled, as if at the idea of going thirty or forty miles for the flour and beans.

A brief quotation from my diary gives a kind of threadbare stereopticon of a trans-Canada journey in winter:

Take of wheat stubble and Hungarian partridges, ten parts. Add a touch of wolf willow, some popple, and three flat cities on a prairie. Sprinkle with moose tracks and Hudson's Bay Scotch whiskey. Flavor with the odor of spruce trees and frozen lakes, Lake Winnepeg goldeyes to taste. Goldeyes resemble whitefish in shape, weigh about a pound, and are taken in Lake Winnepeg, and the Red River which flows from it.

Augment the dog teams, tumplines and canoes of Ontario with the dugouts, packboards and saddle horses of British Columbia. Insert two prospectors panning gold in the Thompson River, one cold cowboy herding whitefaced Herefords west of Jasper, Alberta, and seventeen weird-looking totem poles. Cover the western portion with the twelve-thousand-foot granite peaks of Yellowhead Pass in the moonlight. Drop in two mountain lions, a thousand jack rabbits and some sheep. Mingle with interesting conversation concerning a hot-box in a town called Boston Bar. Spice heavily with Chinamen, and with Indians in Siwash sweaters and derby hats, the squaws mainly barrel-shaped. Garnish with Royal Mounted Policemen who have had more strange adventures than any organized group on earth. Subtract the only unpleasant note in the whole picture—a Vancouver oyster. Compared to the Cotuit oysters of Cape Cod, the Vancouver specimens are tiny wads of wet newspaper.

Illuminate the last two nights with northern lights. Stretch a Chinook arch from North to South on the western horizon. Look from the righthand window— to the North, and partake of some haunting, sober thoughts about the wildfowl that will return in Spring —and suddenly, rather sadly, you hear the conductor shout: "Vancouver! All change!"

But I am neglecting Mr. Pottidge's earlier work. *"Persons visiting Vancouver Island,"* he says on page 90, *"should first see the great city of Vancouver."*

In my case, there were three prime reasons for doing this: (a) A chance to visit Mr. A. Bryan Williams,

Fish and Game Commissioner of British Columbia. He told me some astounding and veracious tales of his men's adventures with wandering Indian tribes in the land of the Midnight Sun; of mad trappers, of superstitions, of frost bitten lungs. (b) A visit to Hartley & Heywood's Sporting Goods store, where Mr. Hartley showed me an original edition of the late F. M. Halford's *Stream Entomology and Fly Tying*. I pored over these hallowed volumes with something akin to fanatic reverence. Countersunk in the handset, beautifully printed, thick white pages, are actual trout flies tied by Mr. Halford's own magic fingers. Some of his drawings and water colors of stream insects are alleged to have laid their eggs one May evening, danced and died. Eagerly I priced the volumes. "Four hundred dollars," murmured Mr. Hartley. I bought some steelhead flies, some stout leaders, an HDH King Eider line and dolefully departed.

(c) The third reason for visiting Vancouver is that you experience the perfect zero-zero situation in fog and rain. By comparison, the renowned pea-soupers of the Maine coast constitute superb flying weather. Hurrying over to Pier D, I embarked with some misgivings on the night boat bound for Victoria, the city at the southern tip of the island. Night and fog mean nothing to the navigators of the British Columbia coast. But let Mr. Pottidge get in a word:

"Victoria is the capital of British Columbia. It is a city of about fifty thousand (50,000) population."

In the light of subsequent friendships, I stumble over the word "population." It cannot be used to define Victorians, because it brings to mind a lot of straw hats and yelling, or a flashlight picture of prizefight attendance. I dearly wish Mr. Pottidge could have met Major A. Gerard Bolton, or Jimmie Gray, or John Hart, or Bill MacIntosh, or Major L. C. Rattray. These gentlemen are not population. They are a race of people. But wait!

The loneliest sound in the world has been called the voice of the timber wolf echoing in a frozen forest. A close second is a loon wailing on a wilderness lake. But for an all-time record, I submit Christmas carols in the ears of a stranger three thousand miles from home.

Then—one right after another—I began to meet fishermen and majors. In Victoria, I believe they are practically synonymous. But first I met George Warren, who is a publicity man, and George introduced me to Major A. Gerard Bolton, and from the instant of shaking hands with Gerry Bolton, I was no longer homesick. Gerry is one of the things in this life that you can't put in writing. But here are a few of the people he reminds you of: Baron Munchausen, Falstaff, Friar Tuck, the (then) Prince of Wales, and Huckleberry Finn with an English accent. Gerry has

an enormous quantity of fly rods and personality, together with an absorbing tragedy involving a large
steelhead trout and the Cowichan River.

Things began to move with what I suppose is un-
British rapidity. Gerry put me up at the Union Club,
and I said a wordless and gloomy farewell to the lobby
of the Empress Hotel and its Christmas carols. Then
he began—rather furtively, I thought—to tell me
about his big steelhead. But he was just lengthening
line, so to speak, when in popped George Warren. And
George spirited me away forty-five miles to the town
of Duncan. I am glad to refer again to the *Insular
Report.*

"The Island," avers Mr. Pottidge, *"boasts many
fine automobile roads."*

If this is so, I am going to take my mentor literally
and agree that the island is boasting. I say this without
spleen, after navigating the aerial switchbacks and
roller coasters of the Malahat in George Warren's car.
There are places on the Malahat where, with a small
amount of blasting, two baby Austins could pass. I am
publicly grateful to George for not running off the
cliff where the sign said "1200 feet to the Bay." It was
a beautiful drive.

At 3:00 P.M. in the hamlet of Duncan, I came face
to face with Major L. C. Rattray—a remarkable man.
Major Rattray is so British he makes you think of

Yorkshire pudding, chutney and the situation in India.
His manner of speaking is reminiscent of the pouring
of concrete, and he doubts nothing that he says. He
has a way of glaring and abruptly drawing in his
breath in a kind of hiss which permanently settles all
arguments in his favor. I have since experimented
with his technique, but to no avail. I suspect one must
be born that way. The Major is one of the best hosts,
and certainly the best fly-fisherman I have ever seen.

He drove me to his bungalow on the banks of the
Cowichan River—a distance of eight miles into the
wild country back of Duncan. Rounding a steep turn
in the narrow road, you see smoke rising from a chim-
ney. Two big Irish water spaniels charge out to greet
you. Behind the house, Douglas firs reach to unguess-
able heights. The house itself fronts on the Cowichan
—deep, green, swift, strangely fascinating. It was in
flood.

On the porch was a cougar skin, a neat pile of split
wood, and three rods. One of these was a prawning rod
fashioned of greenheart by a Scottish artisan. The
other two were English salmon rods, two-handed,
beautifully made.

We had home-cured ham and curried eggs for dinner that evening, and we sat up till all hours sipping
Scotch and water. The Major's information on almost
all subjects, but especially on sport, was astounding.

He could quote pages of facts and theories from Calderwood, Skues, LaBranche, Embody; and I think he had fished nearly *all* of the world's famous rivers. I listened, feeling limp and inferior. The Irish water spaniels had the temerity to sleep.

Next morning, with the season and the condition of the river against us, we rigged our rods for a try in the long pool in front of the house.

At once I learned two things: my five and one-half ounce Leonard was far too light for such powerful water; and Major L. C. Rattray approaches perfection as a fly-fisherman. By means of the Spey cast, he got out a tremendous length of line. The method on steelhead is similar to that advocated for Atlantic salmon fishing with a wet fly. In other words, the current does most of the work. After a cross-stream cast, the line is allowed to curve downstream, turn and straighten. Little, if any, motion is imparted to the fly. Like the Miramichi salmon, the Cowichan steelhead usually strikes just as the line is straightening below you. On one of these casts, the Major's rod twitched, and he brought the tip up sharply. I saw a heavy fish turn a silvery side to the surface. The Major had him on for a minute, and his line went slack. Missed! Getting even one rise from a steelhead in a flooded river near the first of January—even on Vancouver Island —is either very good luck, or very good fishing. The

day before I arrived, Major Rattray had taken two fish
of "about 'alf a stone each."

We cast fruitlessly for an hour before abandoning
hope, then hiked up the river along the shore. It was a
memorable walk. In less than a mile we flushed mal-
lards and mergansers in huge clattering flocks; seven
bevies of willow grouse; four of valley quail; and
what the Major called "a plethora pheasants." We
passed beside a forest of cedars, any single tree of
which would, I estimated, be sufficient to shingle the
entire roof of the Grand Central. Occasionally, in
small tributary streams, we saw the remains of salmon
which had spawned and died, and I couldn't help feeling disappointed in the Almighty for originating such
a wanton scheme.

"*The Island*," asserts Mr. Pottidge in his *Insular
Report*, "*is served by the Esquimalt & Nanaimo R.R.*"

It was to this railroad that I entrusted body and soul
for the return trip to Victoria, Gerry Bolton and further mad references to his gigantic steelhead trout.
Aside from superb views of blue, fir-bordered bays, my
memory of the trip down is dim. But there was this
bit of dialogue with a friendly Scotch trainman.

"Nice to see the sun," I said.

"It is that," he replied. "Are you from the States?"

"Yes, but going native fast," I told him, with an old
London accent filched from Major Rattray.

"I 'ear 'ow employment ain't so good down there yet but wot Congress is puttin' through still another opprobrium," he observed, and I had never heard a tax appropriation described in just that way.

I spent my first night in the Union Club, and at once noted that Victoria has the longest bathtubs in the world. They are of a capacity in excess, I am sure, of the breakfast coffee cups in the Harvard Club of New York. And the average Victorian's bath towel is the approximate size of a four-point Hudson's Bay blanket. Moreover, in Victoria, sea gulls instead of pigeons light on your window sill.

Gerry came around for me next noon, and I could tell by his eyes that he was ripe for unburdening. He said he had "a steelhead-ache," and I knew it was but a matter of time until he began again about the trout. We sat down in green leather chairs. On a nearby table was a little bell shaped like a turnip. Gerry tapped the bell, which reminds me once again of Mr. Pottidge's *Insular Report*.

"Vancouver Island is noted for its fine water supply."

This statement is probably authoritative, but a poised steward, in answer to Gerry's ring, drifted by our table and in his wake left two glasses containing not water, but a bizarre, greenish liquid. "What's this, Gerry?" I asked.

Gerry explained: "It's composed of ingredients."

I took a hesitant sip, and found that a warm glow suffused me, and it seemed after a while that all men were friends. Gerry filled and lighted his pipe. A singularly intense look came into his dark eyes. "About that trout," he began. "It was, as I have said, a steelhead, and Major Rattray took you within a quarter mile of the very spot where it all happened."

"Where what happened?"

Gerry paused so portentously that I wished I had remained mute. I remember wondering at the time if others before me had interrupted him, and set him permanently against interruptions as a whole.

"Major Jimmie Gray was fishing a hundred yards below me," he began again. "I could see the sun glinting now and then on his backcast. It was a wonderful day—cool, windless, not too bright. The Cowichan was clear as glass, and you had to use a long line and fine leader for results. I was using a Dusty Miller, often good for steelhead, on a twelve-foot leader. I dropped the fly close under the far bank of the river, and it was looping down, holding well in the channel of the run, when all at once—"

Gerry stopped in mid-sentence, just when I was sure something cataclysmic was in the offing. His face was a perfect definition of chagrin. "Well," he trailed off, "it's no use going on now. Here comes Jack Rithet,

Charlie Wilson, and John Hart from Government House. You'll have to listen to a lot about snipe and grouse shooting, and bird dogs."

I mumbled something sympathetic, and a moment later was engaged in conversation with the other Victorian gentlemen. We traded episode and information. Jack Rithet, who turned out to be a Yale man, told an anecdote about Ted Havemeyer who is so tall that he is said to have crossed the strait of Juan de Fuca without filling his waders. This brought us back again to fishing, and Gerry leaned forward like a man preparing to run against a storm.

"I was just telling about that steelhead," he said, giving Jack and Charlie a supplicating glance. "I had come to the point where—"

Without a word, as if by prearrangement, the three newcomers arose, bowed, and with military dignity, departed. Gerry covered his face with his hands, took one of them away, smote the bell mightily, and muttered something about a prophet having no honor in his own country.

"Go on," I urged. "Let's hear the story."

But the artist in him had been crushed, despite the fact that my curiosity was by this time genuinely vibrating.

During the next week I became more and more amazed at the variety of fish and game offered the sportsman on Vancouver Island. Gerry piloted me to tiny bays where were a dozen different kinds of ducks, Canada geese and snow geese. Each night we dined at his home, and retired afterwards to his den. Two men could barely squeeze in through the duck and goose decoys, wading gear, collapsible boats, tackle boxes, rifles and guns (Purdys!).

Once or twice I thought Gerry was going to begin again about the steelhead, but he didn't. We were too busy flushing snipe behind Jack Rithet's dogs, watching valley quail, visiting the island's game farm. We went again to the Cowichan, and I took a small cohoe salmon on a red and white bucktail with silver body and red wool tag. This fly represents the candlefish on which the salmon feed. On a tributary stream we discovered a pool where rainbows were spawning, larger rainbows than I dreamed existed in such numbers. Several of them would run between five and six pounds, I guessed. I stood there peering out under the branches of a small cedar, in an attitude of awe and disbelief, wishing it were May or August.

Before I knew it, time came for my departure. In my room at the Union Club, I was morosely packing a pair of wet waders in my bag. It was eleven P.M., and the Vancouver boat sailed at midnight. I managed to get the waders tucked away, and was fitting aluminum fly boxes into small open spaces, when I became aware that Gerry was telling about the steelhead. I didn't turn around or display surprise. I simply tiptoed across the room and locked the door.

Gerry's voice was subdued, like that of a man who is face to face with the Infinite. "When he struck," he said, "it was as if someone running as fast as he could, had snubbed up short on a rope. I was the one who had been snubbed. Nothing could have been more abrupt, more spectacular. Jimmy Gray must have heard the yell that came from me. In a partial daze, I knew he was running in my direction."

At this point I clumsily dropped a hobnailed wading shoe. Gerry winced, but continued: "My reel let out a screech. The line ripped away from it, and my rod waved as if it had the tremors. Straightening up, I tried to follow the fish, floundering my way down toward Jimmy."

Gerry had paused again. He licked his lips, as though all words he could bring to bear were in some way distasteful. "In dreams," he began once more, "have you ever had the sensation of running? Or—no, that's not it at all. Have you dreamed that you had fallen, nude, from a great height, into a net of barbed wire held at the corners by ladies?"

"No."

"Well, anyway, that's how I felt. You see, when a steelhead runs upstream, you've got a chance, light leader or no. But when he starts down, it makes a man wish for belief in the efficacy of prayer. I don't know how I managed to run so fast on those stones—probably inspired, superhuman—but all at once I glanced along my line and saw I was downstream of the fish. Then I got a brief flash of the fish himself. A sort of heliograph informing me that hell was merely warming up. The trout was—well, he was a yard long!"

Gerry stopped, swallowing painfully, as if he had a pickerel bone stuck in his throat. Moisture glistened faintly on his forehead, the first minute beads. "You don't believe me! You doubt me!" he said, huskily.

"No!" I insisted. I realized that no such gleam in a man's eyes could have its foundation in falsehood. "But time's getting along, Gerry. We ought to be getting down to the boat."

Mechanically Gerry followed as I unlocked the door. Mechanically he helped me with my baggage and rods. Mechanically he walked beside me toward the pier, all the time continuing his tale.

"You forget almost everything when you've hooked a steelhead," he muttered. "You forget home, duty, wife, children. You must concentrate. All I can remember of my surroundings during the playing of this fish was a Douglas fir standing on a high bluff with a white cloud back of it. When you're whirled 'round and 'round until you're dizzy, one thing in the circle catches your eye each time around. When you're coming out of ether, your eyes always seem to focus on one certain spot. Well, that was the way with the Douglas fir."

We had passed the Empress Hotel and were turning down toward the pier, where the steamer loomed dark and alive. "It must have been longer than half an hour," Gerry was saying, "before I saw the splice where my casting line joined the backing. Jimmy Gray was right beside me. Usually Jimmy is calm. He piloted a bombing plane with me during the war, and you have to be calm to pilot bombing planes. But now he was not calm, and that made me more excited than ever. Jimmy, holding the landing net, was peering down into the water. 'Should have brought a gaff,' he said, pessimistically.

"That didn't help—Jimmy's saying a thing like that at a time like that. Just then, I saw the knot where my leader joined my line. Then, full view for the first time, the fish!"

Somehow, with no sensing of reality, we had moved across the dark landscape, through a long resounding corridor, up the gang plank and onto the boat. A steward took my bags to my stateroom, and Gerry and I leaned against the starboard rail staring into the black Pacific. Gerry's voice seemed to give the whole picture a tone of dank magnitude, as he went on:

"I turned to Jimmy and said: 'Look!' Did you ever happen to notice what enormous dramatic significance a man can get into that word?"

"No."

"Well, Jimmy Gray did. He looked, and the net began to wobble in his hands, and he said something about a gaff again. Then he said: 'Steady, Gerry old chap. It's a record steelhead.' And the previous record for steelhead, if you'll recall, was—well, still is—held by Homer Marsh, who, on June fifth, 1920, took from East Lake, Bend, Oregon, a twenty-two pounder, which was thirty-nine inches long, with a girth of—"

The gloomy whistle of the steamer announced that we would be sailing in five minutes. Apparently Gerry didn't hear it at all. In fact, he continued talking right through the blast, which endured nearly a minute. I had to pick him up in mid-sentence, several climaxes later—

"—as if I'd been in a wrestling match. My hat was gone, long ago. Somewhere in the melee I'd shipped a cargo of Cowichan River water. I was a little dizzy, and my rod arm was numb to the shoulder. But I could see the leader knot again, now just a foot or so from my rod top. Jimmy leaned forward with the net. He held it low in the water, and I eased the fish over it very slowly. Lying across it, the steelhead extended a foot or more over the rim on both sides."

Someone rattled the chains of the gang plank with a sound like the coming of Marley's Ghost. It began to look as though Gerry would not get ashore, but a tall man with an iron face and a uniform resembling armor got him by the elbow and led him backwards to the main companionway. As he turned to descend, Gerry shouted: "It was a beautiful fresh-run fish—silver, gleaming—" The tall man tugged, and Gerry disappeared. He reappeared in a few moments, standing on the pier, looking up at me, and gesturing fiercely with his hands.

"Jimmy got him out of water—that is, partly. You could see the sun glancing on him, and—"

Brutal, oblivious, brazen, the throaty moan of the whistle cut Gerry short. The engines throbbed from the depths of the steamer, and the pier seemed to be drifting farther and farther away. I could still see Gerry. He appeared to grow smaller in stature as the steamer gathered headway, but mightier in spirit. I am reminded, albeit grotesquely, of something Mr. Pottidge wrote in his *Insular Report*. He tried, it seems to me, to sum up the entire drama of Gerry's steelhead —the hopes, the thrills, the joys and frustrations, the lakes and the rivers of this fisherman's Elysium, when he wrote succinctly:

"*One of the major industries of Vancouver Island is salmon canning.*"

Would I be too presumptuous if, paraphrasing broadly, I said: "The industry of one of the Majors of Vancouver Island is steelhead fishing"?

Ponderously, with a kind of dreadful authority, the steamer was moving out, and I had not said farewell to Major Gerry Bolton! I tried to do it with my eyes and my hands, from the starboard rail. I tried one shout, but it issued from my lips in the form of a bleat, and nearby passengers regarded me in alarm.

The Pacific sent small swells against the sides of the steamer. Gulls wheeled and screamed in the searchlight beams. The whistle again, deep, growling, forbidding, added a final note to departure's bedlam—a bedlam through which, in Gerry's clear, far-reaching voice, I heard the words which brought his story to its inevitable conclusion: *"We lost him!"*

Lights swept by, shore lights and the riding lights of little ships. On the dock, Gerry Bolton was a small retreating figure, lonely in the night. All at once I felt that, besides home, there would be but one place in the world for which I could ever be homesick—Vancouver Island.

On page 302, Mr. Pottidge describes this enduring sentiment in two words: THE END.

SONG OF SOLOMON

Sunday, early October, 1901. The main street of Black Haw, Mississippi, is deserted save for a despondent mule and one Hercules Cadey, a human derelict enthroned on a keg. From a vine-matted pea field comes the high hopeful call of a bob white. And there is the curious, almost inaudible sound which lingers adjacent to all great rivers, for none however deep or slow shall be soundless.

On either side of the main street are weathered houses with smoke lazing from their mud and brick chimneys. Separated by a livery stable, a blacksmith's shop, and a decadent branch of the Mississippi River Steam Navigation Company, are three churches: Methodist, Baptist, and Presbyterian. The churches of Black Haw are poor. They have no pipe organs, no stained glass, no gilded allegories upon their walls. But the congregations make it up to the Almighty when they "sing without further reading" from their musty church hymnals.

This was a crucial Sunday, in that Reverends Bracken, Gurdin, and Redding—unbeknownst to one another in their separate edifices—had simultaneously called their flocks together in song. There was something truly Olympian in the conflict.

"Praise God from Whom All Blessings Flow," intoned the fervent Methodists. Baptist brethren and sistern vied with "Lead Kindly Light," while Reverend Lee Redding's Presbyterian flock lifted up their voices and sang "Mine Eyes Have Seen the Glory of the Coming of the Lord." High over all, shrill and yearning, rose the soprano of Miss Dimity Tredgold, Presbyterian spinster. She lent a terrifying dissonance by establishing and holding her customary half-beat lead over less ambitious singers; and, coming down the home stretch with "as we go marching on," she caught her breath and made a second clarion finish in unison.

The general effect was startling. Out in the street, Hercules Cadey smiled an heretical smile. The mule wobbled its troubled ears. And lo! At the most fervid peak of the discord, down the middle of the main street came Colonel Sherm Applegate, mounted, fourteen jaded fox hounds at heel.

Dogs in general, and fox hounds in particular, are possessed of a network of sympathetic nerves which induce vocal response to certain sounds. These sounds include the whine of the accordion, the convivial rendering of "Sweet Adeline" on courthouse steps at midnight, and the wailing of assorted hymns.

So it came about that old Solomon, the Colonel's most dependable hound, shook himself by sections and, by some obscure muscular process denied man, altered the location of his ears and looked worried. Banjo, a black, white and tan, limped over to the Methodist church lawn and sat down in an attitude of woe and permanence. Others of the fourteen tried and true followed suit in individual style. It was considerably more ominous than the gathering of clouds.

Then did old Solomon in his wisdom hoist his long nose and roll his bleared eyes toward heaven. His jowls trembled. His flews appeared to draw and tighten, and he made of his mouth a round gray-whiskered orifice. The casual listener would have been nonplussed at the volume of sound which issued from that forty-three pounds of dog flesh. It was glorious, if unrighteous, work. He howled down the ultimate verse of "Lead Kindly Light" and was just getting his second wind when the others of the fourteen chimed in, giving tongue impartially for Methodist, Baptist, and Presbyterian.

"*Heel!*" roared the Colonel, sitting rod-straight on his horse. "Solomon! Banjo! Nemesis! Heel!" It was a losing battle from the start, and at length the Colonel's voice trailed off into an unsanctified chuckle.

Thus it came about that the church-goers, as they filed into the main street, beheld the stalwart old man shaking with mirth amid a galaxy of mourning hounds. In straight scripture language, "a sound of great battle was in the land, and of great destruction."

Something had to be done. Hercules Cadey saw this at a glance, and, rising to the emergency, offered his unregenerate assistance in reorganizing the pack. So the Black Haw worshipers and their three reverend leaders observed the Colonel and Hercules working shoulder-to-shoulder, like brothers—and, as humans will, drew hissing and libellous conclusions.

"Hah! Colonel Applegate consorting with a heretic and drunkard! Hah! Haven't we always said—?" And it was true that the Colonel was a stranger in their midst. He had held himself aloof for the two years since he had taken over the old Fernwood plantation. Moreover, he had come to them from "Natchez-under-the-Hill," and therefore by the godly men of Black Haw was initially branded with the mark of Cain.

The affair of the fox hounds shook the morals of Black Haw to the core, and was the direct cause of the clergy calling on the Colonel that evening. They found him in his study sipping from a tall glass which they were positive smelled of rum and cinnamon, thus bearing further upon his unhallowed reputation.

The Colonel, in fact, barring only Hercules Cadey, was Black Haw's most clouded soul. But the citizenry knew all about Mr. Cadey, and nothing at all about Colonel Sherm. They had to guess, for as yet no one had crossed his threshold save old black Tobe, certain favored fox hounds, and the grocery man.

However, an itinerant patriarch once claimed to have seen the Colonel back in the dim sixties in the saloon of the *Southern Planter*, a renowned side-wheeler which had plied between Memphis and N'Awlins. From this point, rumor thrived, grew fat, and was never chased down. "He was a wild one," gossip whispered. "I knowed a man what knowed a man what seen him oncet. He'd engage ary stranger in conversation, draw poker, or a pistol duel. Smoked long Louisiana cheroots, he did. Wore a brace of cap-an'-ball Colts, a reg'lar gold hawser of a watch chain, an' an Old Testament beard." Even though no native Black Hawian had ever laid eyes on the man what had knowed the man, this rumor gratified the curious. It became incorporated as fact in the lore of Black Haw —and the word had been tolerably strengthened on this unfortunate Sunday. . . .

That evening in his leather chair the Colonel sat distinguished and aloof as an oil painting, his face ruddy in the firelight and he regarded the indignant clergymen who called upon him. At his feet, one eye open, lay Solomon, arch-offender and veteran fox-hound. Solomon's character bore a curious resemblance to his master's. Everything Solomon did was on a grand scale. He was a searcher of unknown trails, a swimmer of great rivers, a singer of primordial song on the Sabbath. And he was now, like the Colonel, a firelit hulk sufficient unto himself.

"Be seated gentlemen," said Colonel Sherm.

There was a scraping of chairs, and the Reverend Bracken began his accusation nervously. "Colonel, we have come to ask you not to engage in fox hunting on Sunday—"

"Indeed," said the old man. "So I reckoned."

"That is, in such a way as to again disrupt divine worship in Black Haw. We demand, sir, that you keep your heresies to yourself."

Each of the three clerics felt that at any moment the Colonel might rise, roar, and smite them asunder. Yet bravely they had come, and bravely they would remain to see Justice. Those were solemn years, and the devout brethren were quite certain that the Colonel was a devil to be cast out. And while they waited his wrath, they were vaguely puzzled and vaguely relieved when he greeted their rebuke with an apple-cheeked smile, and a quotation from their own hard-won scripture: "Gentlemen, I am right sorry for what has happened. But I say unto you, that whosoever is angry with his brother without a just cause shall be in danger of the judgment."

At this instant Solomon's pagan tail smote the floor a couple of times. To the brothers, it sounded suspiciously like canine approbation.

"But," persisted the Reverend Gurdin, "you do not attend church."

"In my own way, and in my own time, I do suh," replied the Colonel.

"Yet on the Sabbath you frequently hunt foxes, and the Book says 'thou shalt not kill.' "

"My dear Mr. Gurdin," responded the old man, "the Book sayeth elsewhere that 'Archelus drew his sword and hewed Agag in pieces before the Lord.' And I must enlighten you further, suh: no gentleman would even dream of killing a fox."

The three clergymen found themselves gradually falling under the spell of the Colonel's charm and personality, something they had not foreseen. Was it possible that rumor had misinformed them? It was borne upon them that he was not at all a demon, a duelist, and a doer of evil; but instead a rather pleasing composite of General Robert E. Lee and Moses. Departing, each secretly wished he might number the old man among his flock, for he who converted Colonel Sherm Applegate would indeed be a prophet with honor in his own country.

[165]

But only one of the clergymen—young Lee Redding—returned. It was several evenings later. "I hope I'm not intruding, Colonel."

"Heaven bless you, no, son! No. Take a chair. That one by the desk is right comf'table. Fits a man's back. There now. What's on your mind?"

"Well, questions and apologies, mostly." The lamplight shone on Lee Redding's hair; and on his lips was a forlornly fetching smile. "You see we should have known you didn't deliberately interrupt our services. I—I guess the singing was rather poor, and the hounds knew!"

"Cou'se—it's all right. My sakes. Pure misfortune, all around."

"You told Mr. Gurdin that in your own way you attended church. What—exactly—did you mean?"

The Colonel swept some cheroot ashes from his vest, trifled with his watch chain, and dropped his long blue-veined hand to Solomon's head. "Well, I'll try to tell you. First place, I'm—le's see—twice as old as brother Gurdin and brother Bracken. And I reckon three times as old as you."

"Yes. That's right."

The difference between their ages and their wisdom was so great and so apparent, that the Colonel caused no atom of offense when he added: "So, in the first place, I would likely seek my inspiration elsewhere."

Both men smiled. Solomon thumped his tail. They all got on famously; and along toward the end of the evening they were exchanging opinions on life, the Democratic Party, and horse racing.

"But you haven't explained," said Lee, at length, "just where you find your inspiration or fill your spiritual needs. Is it from books?"

"Partly," said the Colonel, "but—tell you what: You be here in riding togs next Saturday at sunset, and maybe I can show you."

Six miles back of Black Haw, Mount Bedford rears its lofty crest upwards of sixty feet above sea level. Visiting New Englanders would call it a hill, Westerners a knoll, and Alaskans nothing at all. But Mississippians point to it with pride, saying "mountain," and mountain it shall be.

A smoky dusk. In a glade on the mountain top among the black oaks and hickories is a tiny fire, loafingly alive. Two horses and a mule are tethered near by. Colonel Sherm Applegate and young Lee Redding squat close to the fire, boot and buckle gleaming. They are silent and at peace, ruminating upon the sturdy meal of pones and fried pig cooked recently over the coals by old Tobe, the Colonel's aged man servant.

Couched in shadow, coupled in twos or threes, and lying as if in a state of suspended animation, are the famous pack of fourteen. Trig, Walker, July, Bird-song as to breeds. An eye twinkles in the firelight. A cold nose snuffles. An ear twitches. Over all sweeps the glance of Colonel Sherm Applegate, connoisseur of dogs and men.

"Tobe," said the master, beckoning the old servant to him, "uncouple Solomon, Damyankee, and Liza."

Tobe, who was the color of charcoal at midnight, had been awaiting this order in a jittering fervor which belied his years. He sprang to his feet, circumvented the rear end of the mule, and cried: "Yass *suh!* 'At's the onliest dogs fo' d' strike, Colonel. 'Cause ole Sol'mun, he'll lead d' way to Hebben. 'Deed he will."

"Hush, Tobe," said the Colonel, kindly. "Hush and obey."

From the left hip pocket of his jeans Tobe exhumed a "conjure ball." A conjure ball is a thingumbob vested with supernatural powers for good. It may be composed of anything dear or mystifying to its owner. Tobe's was a nondescript ball of trash including strands of hair from the kinky heads of his erstwhile best gals, a rabbit's left hind toe nail, some sassafras bark peeled during the dark of the moon, a portion of hide from the ear of a shote, a decayed magnolia petal, and something moist and woebegone from the paunch of a river catfish.

Tobe touched old Solomon reverently and passed the conjure ball over him, muttering incantations the while. "Go on 'way fum heah, houn' dawg. Go on, *'way!*"

The three hounds shuffled off into the shadows, theirs to seek and strike the scent of the red fox, theirs to inform the night with their valiant voices. Dusk swallowed them. Distance devoured their velvet footfalls. Around the fireside settled the curtain of smoky stillness which is a humid southern night.

For a long time Lee Redding looked at the darkness, listened to the silence. Then, as if from starry space, came a sound which reached into the heart of him: black men singing on a levee. Through the firelight it came, through the crawling shadows, while the round moon glowed on a far horizon. Voices of blended hunger, pathos, tribulation.

"Go down Moses, awa-a-a-a-ay down,
    in Egypt la-a-a-and.
"Hello, Pharao-o-oh, hello-o-o-o——"

Childlike, simple, altogether profound and stirring. Colonel Sherm peered covertly at Lee Redding, and had the wisdom to be silent. Then abruptly the chant was forgotten in the deep baying of old Solomon, who had struck scent. The eleven remaining hounds sprang into whining animation, and the whole night awoke.

Without remembering just how, Lee had mounted and was riding. He felt the strength of a good horse under him. Wind roared in his ears. A branch smote his cheek, and the blood pounded in his temples. Beside him, or ahead of him, rode the Colonel. Sometimes they would stop and listen: above the breathing of the horses, above the creak of saddle gear, they would hear that primitive voice of the trail which is like no other earthly sound.

How shall one describe it? For the baying of hounds is untranslatable, being not so much a language as a sensation. Yet their clamor reminds the listener of something for which mortals continually search but never find. Kipling tried to describe it in *The True Romance*, and he failed brilliantly:

> "Enough for me in dreams to see
> and touch Thy garment's hem:
> Thy feet have trod so close to God
> I may not follow them."

By each note and quaver the Colonel knew that the trail was hot, or cold, or confused. But it was this vague, almost untenable something which he wanted Lee Redding to distill from the voices. It came to the younger man, carried through the lungs of old Solomon, the leader of the pack. It came as they rode wildly. It came in the wind of their speed, and in the lash of unseen branches. Finally, as they sat blowing their horses, they saw a wraith drift across a clearing touched by moonlight. A red fox!

Lee gasped in his excitement as a moment later came the lean relentless forms of the pack in full cry, old Solomon yards ahead, his voice momentous, penetrating, wild. At three o'clock in the morning they drove the fox to earth—nineteen crooked miles from Mount Bedford!

Horses spent, lolling hounds at heel, they turned slowly toward Black Haw. Lee glanced frequently at the Colonel, a man over seventy who had ridden young man's reckless miles that night! And in the early sunshine he turned to him, and cried: "Why, Colonel! I haven't prepared a thing for meeting! And—and it's Sunday morning!"

The Colonel glanced shrewdly at his new found comrade. "Well, now, let's see: How would this be for a text? 'And he opened his mouth and taught them, saying: Blessed are ye when men shall revile you and persecute you and say all manner of evil against you falsely—' "

"That's it! That's great, Colonel. But—where did you learn so much Scripture? We all believed you a heretic!"

"Heretic? Me? Why, lan' sakes, son! I was Circuit Rider in the lower part of this valley twenty years 'fore you were bo'n. I just took the Fernwood place to spend my old age in peace an' quiet."

"Colonel! Why didn't you tell us before this?"

"I reckon you-all never asked."

Lee looked down on his horse's neck and smiled. "And 'we said all manner of evil against you falsely!'"

Sunday, late October, 1901: Presbyterians of the town of Black Haw, Mississippi, asserted that the Reverend Lee Redding had never delivered a more inspiring sermon. Some even claimed that Hercules Cadey himself would have been irretrievably converted. The ripple of excitement became a formidable wave, however, when the young preacher announced at the close of his service:

"This evening Colonel Applegate will address the Men's Bible Class. His subject will be 'The Song of Solomon.'"

THE OLD MEN LOOK BACK

ALL the windows in the camp were open, and you could hear the hot wind whistling in the screens. That wind came smoking out of the southwest, and I shall always believe Hell lies in that direction. It was 104° in the shade. H. and I lay sprawled in our bunks. H.'s son, J., prowled nervously about the room, saying every now and then: "Oh, come on! Let's get going!"

"Let's get going is something I used to say," H. said. He is rising sixty. I am nearing forty. And J. is just over twenty and can't sit still, even in the heat. It came to me, then, that H. and I had been talking a long time about things we used to do, and loads we used to lug, and distances we had covered on a paddle before the time of outboard motors.

J. stopped beside my bunk and looked down at me with a mock threat in his eyes. "How about it? Are you going today, or aren't you?"

We had planned to go to Fifth Lake Stream for trout that afternoon. I had looked up in the diary, and found it would make my forty-fourth trip in seventeen years. In other words, I had already been over the territory eighty-six times, and I had left a lot of sweat on the Fourth Lake Carry, and had broken my first canoe pole on the stream; and on that heart-rending occasion, I had sworn for the first time in the presence of my wife, and she had understood.

Young J. was naked above the waist and he resembled an animated statue with a sunburn. I looked at him, grinning, and remembering exactly how he felt now: nervous to be off somewhere, map-eating, making a canoe jump upstream, and liking the sweat in his eyes. He had already buried the splintered bones of two good canoes that year—one on the Westfield during a five-foot rise of water; and one on the Quoboag.

Fifth Lake Stream has a couple of lively pitches in it, when the water's right, and I was vaguely concerned about J.'s mad policy which he expresses with his downstream warcry of *"Knife it to her!"* It would be a long walk back, if we stove up our canoe—in fly season. J. had been going about for days without an undershirt, and the black flies had found their way inside the buttons of his outer shirt, and tucked a rumply red seam down his center aisle.

"Do they itch any?" I inquired.

"No. 'Course not. Let's go."

"Maybe Pop will bring in some mail."

J. sighed, and it sounded like a seal blowing. He had lately formed a society, of which he was exceeding proud, and the name of it was *The Militant Bachelors' Association.* "You poor old cripple," he said, now. "You come up here to get away from home, and you're here less than a week, and you're pining away for mail."

H., lying on the bunk next to me, began chuckling. We three came pretty close to making three generations, and he was the oldest, and was probably remembering not only the times when he felt as J. did, but the first times he began to feel old, as I did. In other words, he had a kind of panorama, and could afford to chuckle. I knew I ought to chuckle, too, but I couldn't quite make it. I was thinking—and you can think a lot in a little time—of a packing job in the White Mountains I had had, twenty years ago. . . .

Oh, *how* we used to strut! One time we got word a girls' camp was sending a party to Madison huts, on Mt. Madison, where Baldy and Art Cate and I were caretakers. Baldy and I timed our arrival dramatically, stivering up the Valley Way Trail, 4,000 feet altitude in four miles, with a hundred and fourteen pounds of cement in our packs which we were going to use to point up the masonry. We staggered into the hut just as the girls were eating the supper Art had cooked for them, and ostentatiously shucked off our loads. To our dismay, the girls did not so much as notice us. Crestfallen, we remembered that a hundred and fourteen pounds of cement doesn't look as big as two blankets! We were so exhausted we couldn't even visit with the nice young ladies that evening. We just tumbled into our bunks, and Baldy said: "Love's labor lost," and we slept twelve hours straight. After that, whenever we got word of a girls' camp's arrival, we would get the largest packs we could lay hands on, fill them solid full of shredded wheat, and sail up the mountain. The shredded wheat didn't weigh over twenty pounds, but it did the trick on bulk, and we enjoyed a brief fame as super-men.

In the Appalachian Club files, somewhere, are the wild packing records and trail-time records we made. When they began to build an addition to Lakes-of-the-Clouds hut, above timber line on the bleak shoulder of Mt. Washington, three of us hired out as packers on a basis of a cent a pound a mile. Cement and sand would come up the cog railway to be unloaded either at the gulf tanks, or the summit. Thus we packed on the rocks, either around the Westside Trail, or from the summit down—the blond giant from California, nicknamed Sunkist, Dee Northup and I. At one time, when we were in top trim, we averaged five trips a day, toting a hundred and twenty-five pounds per trip.

Then we went crazy, competing on weights. I made a trip with a hundred and seventy-six pounds, and Sunkist broke all known records with two hundred and twenty-six. It still stands, I believe. Not long ago, in a letter to Sunkist, I enclosed a photograph of my young son. And Sunkist wrote back warily, saying: "He's a nice-looking boy, but he can't be yours. He's got shoes on."

What earthly good did all that do me? I cannot say, except that it is good to remember, and not so good to talk about. Here I was, lying in the heat on my bunk, and secretly objecting to lugging one end of a sixty-five pound guide's model canoe across a comparatively level two-mile portage. There is little glory at such a time in a back injury resulting from a bragging load of one hundred and seventy-six, especially at forty when bragging has lost considerable of its zest.

But here was young J., bending over me with a kind of seamy solicitude, and saying in a voice of dark-brown tenderness: "Oh, you poor thing! Does your back hurt today? So, so, sorry!" In his blue, bold eyes there was pretty good evidence that he didn't really give a damn. But I didn't have to invent a response at the moment, because Pop Thornton got in with the mail, and that was something I wanted badly.

Everything was all right at home. My wife enclosed a letter from my son, which I am quoting for its enthusiastic inaccuracies, and its fourth generation significance.

"Dear Mother:

"We have had a swell week-end, mostly fishing of course. Saturday I went with Donny, and saw two water moccasins, snakes very poisonous. One crawled up Donny's leg when in the meantime Donny was hooking a salmon!!!! We saw a whole pile of eels. The Deerfield River opened Sunday. The limit is twelve inches. I caught three beauties, one was a foot and a half long. The rest were about twelve and a half inches long. Please send this letter to Dad. How are you, and how are the baby? I have been using dry flies for fishing. Never worms. Saturday afternoon we had the biggest catapult fight that's been developed in this school. I was badly injured, being hit with a clothespin about two inches from the eye. The person who shot it was only a foot away when he shot it. It was a lot of fun even though someone was injured, so it was all pretty swell. Love, Jimmy."

So far as I know, there has never been an authentic salmon or water moccasin reported in the neighborhood of Deerfield, Massachusetts, and I lay wondering whether my son would some day develop into a teller of tales. And those "beauties," which at the time I believed were rainbow trout, turned out to be chub!

But he had been accurate about his own skiing skill the previous winter. He had led me a panting chase up

Tuckerman's Ravine on the Sherburne Trail, and on the way down, when I spilled headlong with my skis crossed, he had commented with youthful contempt for old men: "Father, I see you have mastered the 'scissors' Christie!"

These meditations were interrupted by the prowling and pacing J., who said, with a gesture of tearing his hair out: "Oh God! Haven't you finished reading that letter yet?"

I had, but I wanted to read it two or three times more, and it was hot, and my back hurt, and H. said: "If you don't want to go today, don't. There's always tomorrow."

So I said to J.: "Let's pack this afternoon and go tomorrow, early. Will you agree to that, J.?"

I had expected violent objections, not to say physical attack from J., but he is unpredictable. He said: "All right. Come on swimming." We did, and I wrenched my back properly, and didn't dare mention it. . . .

In the morning J. asked H. if he wanted to go with us. H. was old enough and wise enough to say "No *thanks!*" It was even hotter than the day before, and the wind had died, and the flies would eat the canvas off a canoe.

At nine o'clock we were crossing the Fourth Lake carry, and the heat had loosened my abused spine so it didn't hurt much, and I could bend over part way without any important groaning. We put into Fourth Lake, and a head wind sprang up and cut our time down for that six-mile stretch.

The lower part of Fifth Lake Stream was flowed by a logging dam at the foot of Fourth Lake, and we paddled clear up to our camp site and left our duffel. We took to the canoe again, and lugged around Hell's Gate rapids. It's a ledge bottom, and you can't get a pole hold to jam a canoe upstream. In the stern, above Hell's Gate, J. got his pole out and boosted us ahead, singing all the time, the pickle running off his nose, and his towhead the center of a cloud of flies. I helped him in the bow, and wondered whether we'd strike trout above the Night Dam, four miles up.

We came to Smooth Ledge falls, and above that, to High Rolling Tier, and then the long straight pitch to the Hossback pool, and a pitch with an S-turn down through the ledges, that we call Slewgundy Heater. I took the pole in the stern, and J. walked along the Hossback through the shot stumps of the big '21 burn. I knew every inch of stream bottom, every eddy, every riffle, and when J. was looking I'd slip her upstream like a salmon up a fishway, and when he wasn't I'd ease along in the deadwater near shore and talk Old Testament to my aching back. J. took her up through the last rips, and the dam looked good to me.

We rigged up our rods and fished two wet flies to a leader—Wickham's Fancy and White-tipped Montreal, Professor and Pink Lady. We took a few small trout in the dam pool, then launched the canoe into the big deadwater above. "I'll paddle, J. You fish," I said.

"No—*you* fish!"

"No—you. Vacations are short, when you're just a kid."

"Kid!" he exploded. "Why, you don't realize what I've been through. To remain single, with my looks and personality, is a constant struggle."

"I used to say that twenty years ago."

"Aw—you and father are always talking about twenty years ago!"

I took a paddle and knelt in the stern. "Let's go." J. climbed in, glanced around at the sky and the ridges as if he were entirely satisfied to be visiting them for a while, and we shoved off.

We came drifting on a still paddle into the Big Eddy pool two turns above the dam, and J. hooked a good trout on his Wickham's, and hollered: "Chowder! Chowder!" A chowder trout, for some unknown reason, is one which is large enough to require the use of the landing net. This one weighed about half a pound, and we looked three times at his gorgeous color and shape before we creeled him.

Circling the shallow left-hand margin of the pool, I

beached the canoe at the upper end, and we stepped out carefully in a riffle with a rubbly bottom. The water felt good on our knees, as we stood side by side, casting over the pool. We took no large trout here, but we took eight good ones, and they would come in close and dart between our legs, seeking cover, and J. would grab for his leader, and whoop at the trout, saying: "Don't *do* that!"

This is a strange, unorthodox and altogether fascinating kind of trout fishing. It is wilderness trout fishing, where the canoe trip to reach it is three-quarters of it, the game you see adds much, and you come home always with a nice basket, and smelling like a Cree.

We stopped at the Leaning Cedar pool where J. had taken a fifteen-incher the previous June. We couldn't raise a trout this time, and pushed on, whispering when the thought of moose or deer was in our minds, and spoiling this stealth by shouts when a fish boiled under our flies. When time lengthened between rises, J. would shoot at targets, congratulating himself in glowing terms when he dropped his fly in a predetermined spot. "Oh, nice *work*, J.!" he would address himself. "You're a wonder!"

"Well, who showed you how?" I inquired, applying for a measure of his fame.

"You did," he admitted, "and who showed *you?*"

"Your father," I acknowledged.

J.'s flies were trailing in the water. He turned, half facing me. "Say, you know the old man is *good*, too? Absolutely no effort to his casting. The line just—" J.'s eyes enlarged suddenly, as a trout took his dropper. "Hey! Don't *do* that! *Chowder!*"

I turned the canoe downstream, and hung to an alder on the right-hand bank. J. worked the trout for five minutes before I slid the net under him. "He'll go a pound, easy," I said. "Look at the color of him. Like a darn sunset."

"You cast now," J. said. "That's the fish I wanted."

"No—we can both cast."

"How?"

"Well," I told him, "a good man should know how to cast with either hand. I can lefty from here, easily."

I wondered, now, whether I had manoeuvered the canoe into this position in order to demonstrate to J. that I was ambidextrous with a fly rod. I stripped off line and let it coil in the floor of the canoe at my feet. Then I grabbed the alder with my right hand, and began lengthening line with my left, pinching it against the cork grip, and loosening up on the shoot.

"Huh. Pretty good man, aren't you?" J. said.

"I can still beat you casting any day, J."

"What will you have to live for when, inevitably, I beat you even at that?" he asked. "And by the way, how is your poor, broken-down back?"

[183]

I had forgotten all about it, but it began to hurt again. "Terrible," I said. "Feels full of treble hooks."

In the next ten minutes I took two beauties with my left-hand casting, and J. another—all close under the alders where the water ran black below a huge old granite. I looked at my watch, and it was almost five o'clock. "Say, we can get back to camp tonight, if we start soon, J."

"Do you really want to go? After lugging the tent, and everything?"

I thought of H. lying in his bunk at the main camp, thirteen miles away—thirteen good, tough miles. Probably he was reading Santayana's *Sense of Beauty*. I thought of lying in a tent, a rock under my hip, a root in my spine, and no chance to cut fir boughs on the big burn. I knew the wind would die out at sunset, and the mosquitoes would come; and they would bite J., and he wouldn't know it. He'd be asleep, but I wouldn't be asleep. The whippoorwills would keep me awake, in this place where I'd tented out forty-three nights. What was wrong with me, anyway? Why didn't I like it now, as much as I had always liked it? I had spent more nights outdoors probably than J. ever would; and I had loved it, and dreamed about it when the last snow began to melt and the first frogs sang in the foggy swamplands. But tonight, I wanted a bunk in a cabin. And perhaps something more—the pride-feeling of a twenty-six mile day, a round trip under man-power, *my* man-power, from camp to above the Night Dam, and back to camp.

"Sure," I said to J. "Unless you're really anxious to stay, let's go back. We've got fourteen trout, and that's enough."

We went, and down river it was fun with J. in the stern at his pole, and I bow-man. The current, even the white parts, wasn't fast enough or steep enough for J. He would give a great har-oosh with his pole, and you could hear the wind in your ears, and the water-sound, too. *"Knife it to her! Knife it to her!"* he'd yell.

In Hell's Gate, the lower pitch, we hit two rocks hard on the starboard side at the water line, and cut the canvas, but not badly. Below, we picked up our duffel where we had left it, and in half an hour we were feeling the fair wind on Fourth Lake. While the canoe drifted, we ate a can of tomatoes, and some corned beef sandwiches, and watched the sun go down back of Unknown ridge. J. scooped up a few mouthfuls of water over the side, wiped his mouth on the back of his hand, and began singing. Well, they don't call it singing—the young fellows don't. They call it swinging, or scatting.

"Honey, won't you take it slow, shuffle off to Buffalo—" J. sang. I couldn't sing that kind of stuff, so when a break came I sang:

"Baby dear, listen here, I'm afraid to go home
    in the dark.
Every day, so the papers say, there's a robbery
    in the park—"

"Hell!" J. blurted. "If you want a really smoking tenor, sing one that I *know*—one like 'Sweet Marimba, she's long an' limber.' "

We nosed into the Fourth Lake carry about dark, and all you could hear were mosquitoes and bull frogs. We stowed the tent and blanket roll where we could come and get it the next day, and prepared to travel light. "Which end do you want to lug?" J. asked. "Or —out of consideration for your tortured spine—shall I lug it alone?"

We were standing by the canoe, our sweaters tied across our necks for padding. "I've lugged a good many across here alone," I said.

J. made a snorting sound: "Yes, yes, I suppose that was in the old days."

"I'll take the bow," I told him. "Then I can shift shoulders."

We didn't say much going across the carry. It was dark, and I had to watch my footing, and I was winded as an ancient truck horse. Besides, J. was singing: "I hate to se-e-e-e—the evening sun go down," and there was more, about how his "swe-ee-tie, done left the town—"

[186]

But I was thinking: here was the yellow birch blowdown where Little Jim and I had seen the big bobcat; and here the swamp where I had shot partridge; and here the dimming trail back into Unknown Lake. "Eighty-eighth trip on this carry," I thought.

When we put the canoe into Dobsis Lake for the last lap to camp, my ears were singing with tired, and my face felt as if I had to hold it together. But J., in the bow, made the canoe jump forward every time he put his paddle in the water, and he was going through his whole list of hot-songs, radio learned.

When we got to camp, I rose up slowly out of the stern, and unbent my knees, one by one. J. rolled the canoe out of the water onto his shoulder, and carried it across to a rack, where he tied it down in case a squall came up in the night. We cleaned the trout in Pop Thornton's kitchen, and iced them down to take out.

"How do you feel?" J. asked, as we walked across to the bunk house.

"I feel fine, young fellow. How do you feel?"

"Honest," he said, "are you really okay? Because— look—!" J. stopped on the cabin porch, as a new idea got a grip on him.

"Look what?" I asked.

"Well, I was thinking about tomorrow. We could go back over the Fourth Lake carry, and open all the gates on the new dam, see? Boy-oh-boy! That would

give us a regular driving head of water on Fourth
Lake Stream. We'd run the stream, and go on down
through Third Lake, lug into the two Getchell Lakes,
and into Wabassas, and then down Wabassas Stream
into Compass, and—"

"*No!* Double-barreled negative!"

J. leaned against a post in an attitude of supplica-
tion, and said: "Oh, St. Peter, please send me one
sound bow-man for tomorrow, and forever rid me of
travelling with a couple of crippled old coots."

I opened the screen door and pushed J. through, and
closed it quickly behind us to keep out the mosquitoes.
H. was lying in bed reading by lamplight, and he
looked up startled to see us back, but he said: "I *knew*
you'd come!"

"Father," J. began, sitting beside him on the bed.
"How about a little downhill river work tomorrow?"
Then, as he outlined the trip he had lately suggested
to me, his enthusiasm grew. I leaned over carefully
and removed one moccasin, then the other. My back
hurt so I was affronted that it didn't make some kind
of a noise when I bent it. I heard H. chuckling, as J.
finished his plan for a forty-mile trip.

"What's troubling you, Father?" J. asked. "I'm
serious."

"Yes—yes, I know," H. told his son. "I was thinking of the last time *I* made that trip."

"Oh, so you've actually made it, huh?"

"Certainly. Remember, Ed?" he said, looking my way. I nodded, and H. went on, looking with amused tolerance at his restless-footed offspring. "You," H. said to him, "slept most of the time in the bow of my canoe."

"Huh. How old was I?"

"About six, or seven. We had a head wind for the nine miles on Third Lake, and on Compass, too. And on the carries—oh my!"

"What did I do on the carries?" J. asked, apparently hoping for some earlier evidence of his present prowess.

"Nothing. You did nothing at all. I carried you."